Fiona: Forever?

written and illustrated by Erinn Uher

This is a work of fiction. Names, characters, places, and incidents either are the product of the author's imagination or are used fictitiously. Any resemblance to actual persons, living or dead, events, or locales is entirely coincidental.

First edition 2019

Book design by Tobi Carter

ISBN 978-1-7333840-0-1 (paperback)
ISBN 978-1-7333840-1-8 (hardcover)

To every child that's ever felt invisible.

"Have I not commanded you? Be strong and courageous. Do not be frightened, and not be dismayed, for the Lord your God is with you wherever you go."
Joshua 1:9

Acknowledgments

I believe God places certain people in your life on purpose, using them as a tool to help fulfill His plan for you. I believe He gave me my friend, Melanie, knowing without a doubt that she would help me to grow into the woman He created me to be, into the mother He intended me to be. Melanie opened my eyes to the world of foster care and I've been passionate about it ever since.

Over the years, my husband and I have welcomed several children into our home. Some of them moved on to other homes, some went home to their biological families, and a couple of them found their forever home with us. I wish we could have done more, but we simply ran out of room. I'm so grateful for the seasoned foster parents out there, like my friend Melanie, with far more experience than myself, who continue to love and care for all the children that need them. When I grow up, I want to be just like them. Don't you?

Before reading this book, it's important to understand that *Fiona: Forever?* is a fictional story. Fiona's story may not be like yours. It may not be like your friend's or your neighbor's stories. Every child in foster care comes from a hard place.

Every child in foster care comes with their own hurts, their own story- personal to them. Every case is different, with different needs and different outcomes. Hopefully, this story will resonate with someone and open their eyes to a greater need. Hopefully, this story will touch the heart of a hurting child or change the heart of a curious one. Either way, it is just that- a story.

I think everyone has the ability to tell a story. The only tool you really need is an imagination, and perhaps a pencil and some paper. Dreaming up the characters and watching their journey unfold is so much fun. That part was easy for me. Fiona leapt from my mind's eye as if she'd been fighting to get out all along, anxiously waiting to be shared with the world. Night after night, I wrote in the dark as my little boys fell asleep. And night after night, I read my words to my daughter, Frankie. We brainstormed together and fell in love with Fiona together. But still, it wasn't quite ready. Somehow, this story needed to become a book. A real book. And I needed a lot of help with that part.

My family and friends have been amazing throughout this entire process. Thank you, Steve, for encouraging me to pursue self-publishing and for never letting me quit. You believed in me when I didn't. I love you - truly and deeply. And thank you to my beautiful children for being the absolute best kids in the entire world. How could I ever give up, knowing you were counting on me to follow through. I pray you all find your own passions in life and work hard to achieve your goals. If I can do it, you can do it tenfold! I love all five of you with every breath I take. I'm so thankful for my wonderful editor, Mary Auxier of Bluestocking Editorial. Thank you for your honesty and gentle guidance. You were with me every step of the way, always looking for ways to improve my manuscript, helping me to become a better storyteller and more refined writer. Thank you, Mary! A special thanks to all of my beta readers. You all suffered through my early drafts and offered invaluable advice that only improved the story. Thank you for your time, your generosity, and for your priceless feedback. Thank you, Rachel Duchesneau. Your support and your detailed notes were invaluable to me. I am forever grateful! Seriously, friend - you have a gift. And tell those gorgeous babies of yours that book two is already in the works. Thanks for the encouragement and the many, many prayers. You're amazing!

My favorite part of the editing process was watching the videos of Mrs. Kawchak's 2018/2019 second grade class reading my story together. I don't know if I would have gotten this far without those videos. Thank you, Mrs. Kawchak and thank you, especially, to your students. You all played such an important role in bringing Fiona to life and making this book what it is today.

Thank you to my designer, Tobi Carter. I gave you the pieces, all mixed up and scattered, and you worked your magic to turn my jumbled mess into a masterpiece. I can't thank you enough for your help and expertise! You are a rising star in this industry.

And to God, above all, thank You for the gifts You've given me and the family You've blessed me with. I believe You gave me Fiona's story for a reason and I can't wait to see what You do with it. I'll continue to pray for eyes to open and hearts to change.

Contents

Introduction

Peeking through her enormous glasses, hidden under that mountain of red curls, Fiona looks like any normal eight-year-old girl, doesn't she? That's because she *is* normal. She's as normal as normal can be.

Quite normal.

But also kind of special.

While from the outside Fiona may look like an average girl, on the inside, this freckly faced kid is wise beyond her years. Life hasn't been easy for Fiona. Face it, life really isn't easy for any kid. But for a kid growing up in **foster care**, like our Fiona ...

It's a whole different story.

So here it is.

Her story.

The story of Fiona Foster.

Chapter 1
Meet Fiona
June

I *can take care of myself. And I can take care of Melvin, too.* This was what Fiona had always told herself. Melvin was the only living thing Fiona has ever been able to rely on. You see him there? Peeking out of her pocket? They met last winter in the trees behind one of Fiona's foster homes. Melvin got himself trapped in an old bird feeder, as he was hiding from a big hungry hawk. Fiona freed him, but she could not save his poor little tail. Ever since that day, this unlikely pair were inseparable. Fiona made sure Melvin's belly was full, and in return, he lent an ear whenever she needed someone to listen. Melvin was Fiona's very best friend. To tell you the truth, that tailless, fuzzy gray mole was her only friend.

Fiona was on her way to meet the Oliver family. Another family, another house, another everything. Being taxied from one unfamiliar place to the next was one of the few consistent things in this girl's life. Most kids could rely on their family, their routine. Not Fiona. All she could count on were uncomfortable days, short stays, and the anxious car rides that followed.

"I wonder what kind of weirdos these ones will be?" Fiona whispered. She learned at a young age to expect the worst. "Thank God I have you, Melvin. I can always count on you." She barely said the words out loud. No one knew about Melvin, and Fiona wanted to keep it that way. She tucked him down further into her pocket and rested her head on the cold glass.

Through the car window, Fiona watched the tall buildings and busy streets turn into not-so-tall buildings and curiously quiet streets. She saw mothers pushing their babies in strollers and men carefully trimming the shrubbery that lined their yards. A stray cat, or perhaps just a lost one, darted through a field chasing a small blue butterfly.

Mrs. Jones, Fiona's **caseworker**, drove in silence, her worn leather briefcase lay on the seat beside her, the navigation system's robotic voice shouting out directions through the car speakers. Mrs. Jones had been Fiona's caseworker since the very beginning. Fiona liked Mrs. Jones. She was funny and kind and was trying hard to help.

When Fiona was only two years old, **CPS** and the **judge** decided she needed a new family. Although Fiona's **biological family** loved her very much, they were just not able to take care of her and they knew it was in Fiona's **best interest** to voluntarily sign a **TPR**. They lost their parental rights and the courts gave Mrs. Jones the job of finding Fiona a new family. It's been six years of waiting, six long years of wishing. But still no family for Fiona.

"They were sick, Fiona. They worked hard to keep you, to get better. But in the end, they agreed that finding you a new family was best. **Family reunification** just wasn't an option." Mrs. Jones's answer never changed. Fiona used to think about them all the time. She tried to picture them, tried to imagine what they were like back then. Over time, their faces blurred and the memories faded.

"Keep your eyes on the future, Fiona." Mrs. Jones told her one time. "I promise I won't stop until you have a family. You deserve to be happy."

All Fiona ever wanted, all she ever thought about, was a family of her own. "There has to be a place for us, Melvin. Surely we belong somewhere. Don't ya think?" Melvin's paws tickled Fiona's skin as he scurried up her sleeve to rest on her shoulder.

6

"Almost there, Fiona." Mrs. Jones said.

Fiona's heart raced a bit faster as they pulled up to the Oliver family's home. Her stomach did a few flips. She hated this part. Meeting a new family, learning new rules, doing her best to smile and pretend that everything is all right. What if they were mean? Or too nice, even? What if they smelled funny and ate weird food? What if they had a cat? Fiona hated cats because most cats hated Melvin. She could get past strange smells and gross food. But if they had a cat, the deal was off.

Fiona closed her eyes, took a deep breath, and blew it out slowly. Mrs. Jones put the car in park and turned to face her.

"Honey, I really think you will like it here. The Olivers are good people. They can't wait to meet you."

Like I haven't heard that before, Fiona thought. She rolled her eyes and went back to nervously biting her fingernails. Mrs. Jones got out of the car and walked around to Fiona's door. Fiona sat still, waiting as long as she could.

"Ready?" Mrs. Jones tapped her fingers on the rear window.

Fiona held her small bag of belongings tightly against her chest and opened the door, the hot June air smacking her in the face.

"Here we go, Melv," she whispered. "Let's get this over with."

Mr. and Mrs. Oliver were waiting at the door, hand in hand, smiling gently. Newbies. As she followed Mrs. Jones up the sidewalk to the porch, Fiona kept her face down, barely moving, while the adults exchanged polite greetings. Fiona continued to stare at her worn-in red tennis shoes.

"Mr. and Mrs. Oliver, I'd like you to meet Fiona Foster. Fiona, say hello to Pete and Lorraine Oliver. And that's Clyde." Mrs. Jones gestured toward the far corner of the garage.

The teenaged boy stopped shooting hoops to listen in on the introductions. He held the basketball and waved shyly. Fiona snuck a quick glance and immediately shifted her gaze back to her shoelaces. *They seem like okay people.* For now. Friendly or not, Fiona didn't want to be here, and she expected her stay wouldn't last long. Fiona rarely stayed with any family for more than a few months—a year at the absolute most.

"Fiona, can I show you to your room? You can put your things away and rest if you'd like." Lorraine reached out to take the girl's hand but Fiona clutched her bag even tighter, both arms around it in a bear hug. Lorraine gave her a smile and moved her hand to gesture toward the door. Once Fiona stepped inside, the woman led the way through the kitchen and up the stairs.

The bedroom wasn't too small nor too big. A twin-sized bed with a brownish crocheted bedspread was positioned under a window, a dresser stood in the opposite corner near the door. The walls were bare except for one medium-sized picture of a cat and her kittens hanging, crooked.

"I know it's not much, sweetie." Lorraine straightened the picture. "We kept it neutral because we didn't know who would sleep in here. If you'd like, maybe we can paint the walls someday." She smiled. "Our bedroom is at the end of the hall if you need anything and the bathroom is the first door on the right, just before Clyde's room. Go ahead and get settled while we finish up with Mrs. Jones." Lorraine turned and softly shut the door behind her.

"Well, Melvin. What do ya think?" Fiona asked. Melvin climbed down Fiona's clothes and stood on his hind legs on the floor beside her feet. He looked around. Fiona walked over to the picture of the cats. She looked at it closely, studying it with squinted eyes, hoping to like it.

She looked at the picture.

She looked at Melvin looking at the picture.

Melvin shuddered.

"That does it," Fiona said. She would never like cats, and she definitely did not like this picture. She climbed up on the toy box and stood on her tiptoes to take it down without breaking it. Fiona slid the framed picture under the bed and gave her tiny friend a reassuring tap on his head.

"Is that better, little guy?" Melvin squeaked in response.

Fiona and Melvin found the quietest, emptiest corner in the room. She tossed her bag onto the floor and sat down next to it. *This will do.* A special corner, a hidden spot where she could be alone with Melvin. A quiet place where they could stow away, tucked between the dresser and the wall, and dream of a better future.

They sat together in that corner and listened as Mrs. Jones' car backed down the driveway and pulled away. Fiona picked Melvin up from the floor and snuggled him against her cheek. His tiny whiskers tickled her skin.

"It's just you and me, Melv. On our own. Again." Fiona closed her eyes and rested her head against the wall behind her.

Draw the Olivers' house.

Imagine how Fiona felt when she heard Mrs. Jones drive away. Now, think about the Oliver family and how they must have been feeling. How were their feelings similar? How were they different?

Chapter 2
Day Two
Still June

Early the next day, before the sun was awake, Fiona and Melvin huddled together, eyes wide open, under the blanket on the floor. That's right. Fiona slept on the floor, comfortably curled up in her hidden corner. Over the years, she learned to appreciate the commonality of the floors in the bedrooms she borrowed. Floors were firm and cool and didn't vary all that much. Compared to the many different mattresses on the many different beds she's been lent, most floors felt the same when she slept on them.

A soft mattress drove Fiona batty. A springy mattress made her want to pull her hair out. And a stinky mattress? A stinky mattress just made her want to puke. Besides tossing and turning, Fiona wasn't sure why, deep down, she didn't like beds. Maybe she couldn't sleep on them because none of them was ever really hers. Even the clean ones. Who wants to sleep in a borrowed bed, anyhow? Fiona surely did not. Someday, when Fiona finds her forever family, when she moves into her very own room, not a borrowed room, maybe then she'll sleep in the bed.

Fiona rolled onto her side, propping her head up with her elbow. "Do you think Clyde's still mad at me?" she asked her friend. Melvin couldn't talk, but he had his own little ways of communicating with her. His beady black eyes connected with hers. He stood up on his hind legs, reached his front paws up toward Fiona, and squeaked the faintest squeak. He may not answer her as you or I would, but he was definitely listening. Fiona knew Melvin was always listening.

Yesterday was Fiona's first full day with the Olivers, and already she felt doomed. How was she supposed to know the chalkboard was off limits? Why have a chalkboard in the family room if you couldn't use it? She would never have erased it had she known Clyde's grandpa drew that airplane just before he died. When Clyde saw the board and immediately stormed upstairs, stomping loudly, Fiona knew she'd messed up. She didn't know why until later, when she was brushing her teeth and overheard Lorraine and Clyde from across the hallway.

"Honey, she didn't know. I'm so sorry Grandpa's drawing is gone..." Lorraine paused. "It's going to take time, you know, getting used to each other."

"I know, Mom. I get it. I do. I'm not really mad at Fiona. I'm just sad to see Grandpa's plane erased is all. I'll get over it."

Fiona wouldn't have erased it had she known how important it was. She felt terrible about it, but she was also sort of relieved. The quicker she screwed up here, the faster the Oliver's would give her the boot, and then Mrs. Jones could take her to the next place. She'd find the right family, eventually. Wouldn't she?

"What do you think, Melvin? You ready to move on to our next house already?" Fiona straightened the blanket.

She spent most of the morning in the bedroom, laying quietly next to Melvin, listening and learning. She took it all in. Lorraine was the first to wake up and make her way to the bathroom. She closed the door slow quietly but once inside, the shower was loud, and the exhaust fan made a squealing sound that was sure to wake everyone up. Pete, clearly the morning person of the family, hummed loudly while he walked down the stairs and Clyde was a fan of rock music. His alarm clock went off at 7 a.m. playing an old song that immediately sent Fiona back to a time in her life she would have rather forgotten. Back to when she lived with Max and Joni. They loved rock music, too. Fiona hated everything about her time with them. They definitely didn't sign up to be **foster parents** for the right reasons.

Max and Joni's house smelled like cigarette smoke, and the TV was always blasting. They never talked to Fiona, rarely even looked at her. They posted a chore list on the refrigerator every morning, put a box of cereal on the counter, and spent the rest of the day pretending Fiona didn't exist. She was so happy the day she left that little house in the woods. Turns out Max and Joni didn't really want a kid. Mrs. Jones saw through their act and packed Fiona's bag in a rage.

"Fiona needs a family that loves her. Not you pathetic bullies that just make her do your work. **Kinship care** or not, you don't deserve her." She yelled at them then slammed their door behind her, driving away with Fiona in the back seat.

Fiona remembered that day clearly. She opened her eyes, relieved. She wasn't at Max and Joni's cabin anymore. She was at the Olivers' house, in her corner, with Melvin.

"That was the only time I ever saw Mrs. Jones cry. You were the one good thing to come from that place, Melvin." She stroked the fur between her friend's ears. Melvin's whiskers wiggled. His head tilted to the side at the sound of his name.

"You remember the Diner we went to after we left Max and Joni's? The pancakes were bigger than our plates. And you ate most of my bacon!" Fiona giggled. She thought about the phone calls Mrs. Jones made from their corner booth and the strained tone of her voice as she tried to convince Fiona that everything would be all right. They ate a late breakfast and were still there when the lunch crowd thinned out. Hours passed before Mrs. Jones's phone rang.

"We found you a temporary home, Fiona. An older lady that takes kids in for short-term visits. She has an open bed for you. What do you say we get a couple of pieces of pie wrapped up and be on our way?" Mrs. Jones rubbed her eyes and put her glasses back on her face. *Do I have a choice?* Fiona knew she didn't. She went where the courts told her to go.

Why was Clyde upset after Fiona erased the airplane? Why did Fiona feel relieved? How would you feel if someone erased a drawing that was special to you?

Chapter 3

Remembering Miss Alice

The Same June Day

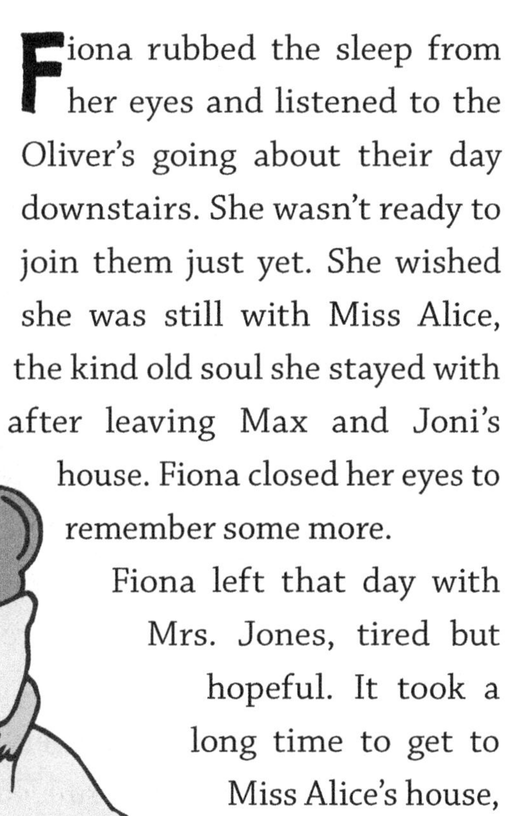

Fiona rubbed the sleep from her eyes and listened to the Oliver's going about their day downstairs. She wasn't ready to join them just yet. She wished she was still with Miss Alice, the kind old soul she stayed with after leaving Max and Joni's house. Fiona closed her eyes to remember some more.

Fiona left that day with Mrs. Jones, tired but hopeful. It took a long time to get to Miss Alice's house, but Mrs.

Jones eventually parked along the curb in front of an old purple home with faded shutters. The yard was small but neatly kept, the porch inviting, and on an old wooden swing sat a short, plump, African American woman with fuzzy gray hair.

She reached out to Fiona. “Shake my hand, girl. I won’t bite ya.” Miss Alice had worn, hard-working hands. And kind eyes. Fiona could see the kindness shining through Miss Alice as clearly as she could see the flowers on the woman’s apron.

Fiona pulled the blanket up under her chin. It felt like a lifetime ago since that day when she shook Miss Alice’s hand for the first time.

“I bet you miss her as much as I do, huh? Especially her cooking.” Melvin was curled in a ball on the pillow next to Fiona’s crazy morning hair. He licked his lips.

Fiona thought about Miss Alice a lot. She wasn’t with her that long, but that kind old lady made a real impact on Fiona’s heart. She had a way of commanding a room, making her presence known and her words heard. Especially outside on her swing. Fiona spent about a month with there, swinging away most of her evenings, listening to Miss Alice share whatever was on her heart. She recalled one conversation in particular that really stuck.

“Come, girl. Sit with me.” Every time she patted the empty side of the swing with her wrinkled hand, Fiona knew she was in for a lesson.

"About forty years ago, I opened that door to my very first child. He came in here like a tornado, tearing up my house and doing his best to try an' tear me down. Back then, I had no idea what I was gettin' into. But you best believe I wasn't 'bout to let no roughneck kid walk all over me. I took that boy by his ear and marched him right up those steps there. Gave him an earful he ain't never forget. It took some time, and a few more of them talks but before long that wild child was brushing his teeth in the mornin', cleanin' up his own plate after dinner and huggin' me tight before bed." Miss Alice continued, "He was just so used to bein' hurt and neglected by the grown-ups in his life. He needed to learn to trust all over again. Needed to know for sure I was gonna be here for him no matter what, even on the ugly days."

Miss Alice pointed to a long row of lines cut into the trim around her doorway. "See those marks up there? The notches in the wood? DJ carved the first one with his pocket knife. I was mad as a hot poker when I saw the damage he done to my poor house. I was fixin' to give him a piece of my mind that day, but then I thought to myself, *Now, Alice, it's only a piece of wood. Ain't even a nice piece of wood.* That boy, DJ, he just wanted to leave his mark on this world, and I suppose he chose to leave it, quite literally, on my porch. You see, girl, he left his mark there," she pointed at the carvings, "and here." Miss Alice rested her hand on her heart."He's all grown up now, got a family of his own. He still calls me couple times a year just to check on me. Calls me Mama Alice." The old lady handed Fiona a small pocket knife. "Now don't you dare cut yourself, girl, but go on over there and put your own mark on that there board. And do a good job of it. Don't you ever question your ability to make your mark on the world, Fiona. You may not have had a choice about where you been, but you can decide where you gonna be. You can choose to be bitter, to fight and be sad like some of the kids I've known. Or you can choose to make the most of the hand you been dealt and rise above it all just like DJ did. It's up to you, girl."

Fiona took the knife from Miss Alice and looked at the notches closely, counting each one as her fingers brushed over them: 47 little grooves, 47 children. Fiona makes 48.

"Why so many, Miss Alice?" Fiona asked.

"That's an easy one, girl. Cause I used to be just like ya'll. I dreamed of the day I'd find my place, my family. I grew up in this broken system. Back then, believe it or not, it was a lot worse. I know what it's like to be lonely. To be hungry. To feel like I was unlovable and unwanted. When I was a young girl like you, I pushed everyone away, so bitter. I was so 'fraid to open my heart up just to be hurt again. Never did find my family back then. When I got older, I realized what a mistake that was and I vowed to make things right. So I opened my heart and made my own place, built my own family right here in this ol' purple house, with all you." She pointed at the carved wood. "I live in the hearts of all of you kids and all you kids live in mine. Long after you leave here to move onto the next part of your journey with your new family, I'll be lookin' at that notch you cut and prayin' for ya, girl. Just like I do for all the ones that came before you."

It felt like a lifetime had passed since Fiona sat on the porch with Miss Alice. But actually, it had only been a few days. She missed the woman with her whole heart. No one ever talked to her like Miss Alice did. Before she left, Fiona promised Miss Alice she would make her mark on the world, a mark the woman could be proud of. This morning, with the Oliver's, Fiona wasn't so sure she was living up to Miss Alice's expectations. *What if I'm just not good mark-making material?*

She hoped that wasn't true, but how could she know?

Miss Alice has provided a temporary home to 48 different children. Her positive impact on the children she cared for is evident in the story of D.J., and we know she left quite an impression on Fiona, as well. Can you think of anyone that has made a positive difference in your life or the life of someone you know? How have you made a positive impact on the life of someone else? What are some ways you could do so in the future?

Draw a portait of Miss Alice.

Chapter 4
Bacon!
Late July

Fiona tried to hide from the bright beam of sunshine stretching across the room, but the curtains were open just enough to let the light creep in and take over. She could hear the birds chirping and the sound of the Olivers starting their day downstairs. It'd been just over a month since she moved in. Overall, it was an okay place to be, aside from a few minor hiccups, of course.

Erasing Clyde's chalkboard.

Spilling a red drink on Lorraine's kitchen rug.

Flooding the bathroom sink, soaking the floor.

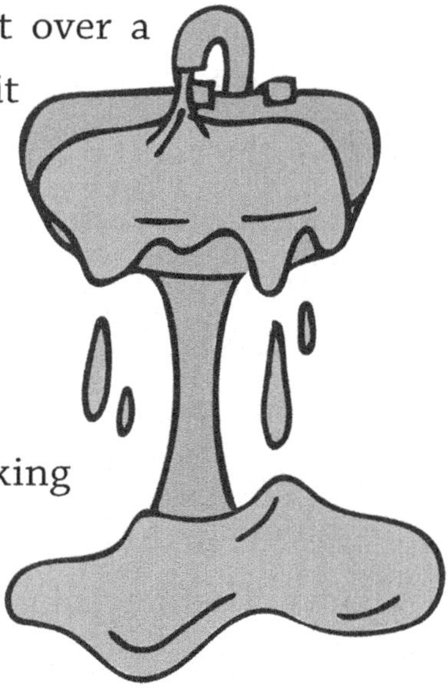

It could be worse. For Fiona, things most definitely have been worse. Slowly, she was becoming more comfortable, spending less time curled up in the corner and more time venturing through the house. Fiona even thought about sleeping in the bed once. But she didn't.

For now, she and Melvin loved to snuggle into their corner and dream of the life they wish they lived: A father to play catch with. A mother who would French braid her hair and teach her to bake cookies. And a bedroom that genuinely belonged to her, complete with a bed she could call her very own and a soft red blanket that no one else had ever used before.

And a real cage for Melvin.

Fiona would set it near a window so he could nap in the warm sun.

He'd love it there.

Anything would be better than his stinky shoebox hidden under the bed.

So often, Fiona dreamed of her perfect family and her perfect house and her perfect life.

"One day, Melvin. One day we will be home forever with a real family and every day will be wonderful." She gave him a gentle pat. "Time to get up, Melv. I really gotta pee!"

Fiona brushed her wild hair and pulled it up into a high ponytail before making a mad dash to the bathroom. Her belly growled as she walked down the stairs toward the kitchen. Melvin's belly growled, too. Bacon! Melvin's absolute favorite food of all. Fiona saw he was already licking his tiny lips.

Today was Saturday. Big breakfast day in the Oliver home. There were pancakes and waffles, French toast and home-fried potatoes, bacon and cheese-covered eggs. Plus, jelly toast, orange juice, and coffee. Fiona sat down in her favorite chair. It was her favorite because it had one loose leg that wobbled to the left side. She always made sure she sat on that chair in just the right way. The wobbly way, of course.

Fiona thought there was way too much food for one family to eat, but Lorraine said she enjoyed cooking breakfast foods the most. And the guys enjoyed eating it all. Especially Clyde.

His plate was already heaping. He sort of ate like a pig, taking huge bites that barely fit in his mouth, shoveling it in faster than he could chew.

Unlike Clyde, Fiona filled her plate with discretion. A piece of bacon for herself and another for Melvin. One pancake smothered in strawberry jam and a small scoop of cheesy eggs. Lorraine poured Fiona a glass of orange juice.

"We have a fun day ahead of us so eat up. We're going to the beach! I packed a cooler with sandwiches and fruit for a picnic lunch. Fiona, do you have a bathing suit?"

"No, Mrs. Oliver. I don't," Fiona responded shyly.

"That's okay. I wasn't sure, so I picked you up a new one at the store the other day." Lorraine handed Fiona a bright colored one-piece bathing suit with rainbow stripes and stars all over it. Fiona thought it kind of flashy, but she didn't say so. "Thank you, Mrs. Oliv...I mean, thank you, Lorraine." She was still trying to get the hang of using their first names like they'd asked her to do.

Pete and Lorraine.

Lorraine and Pete.

And Clyde.

Draw YOUR favorite breakfast foods.

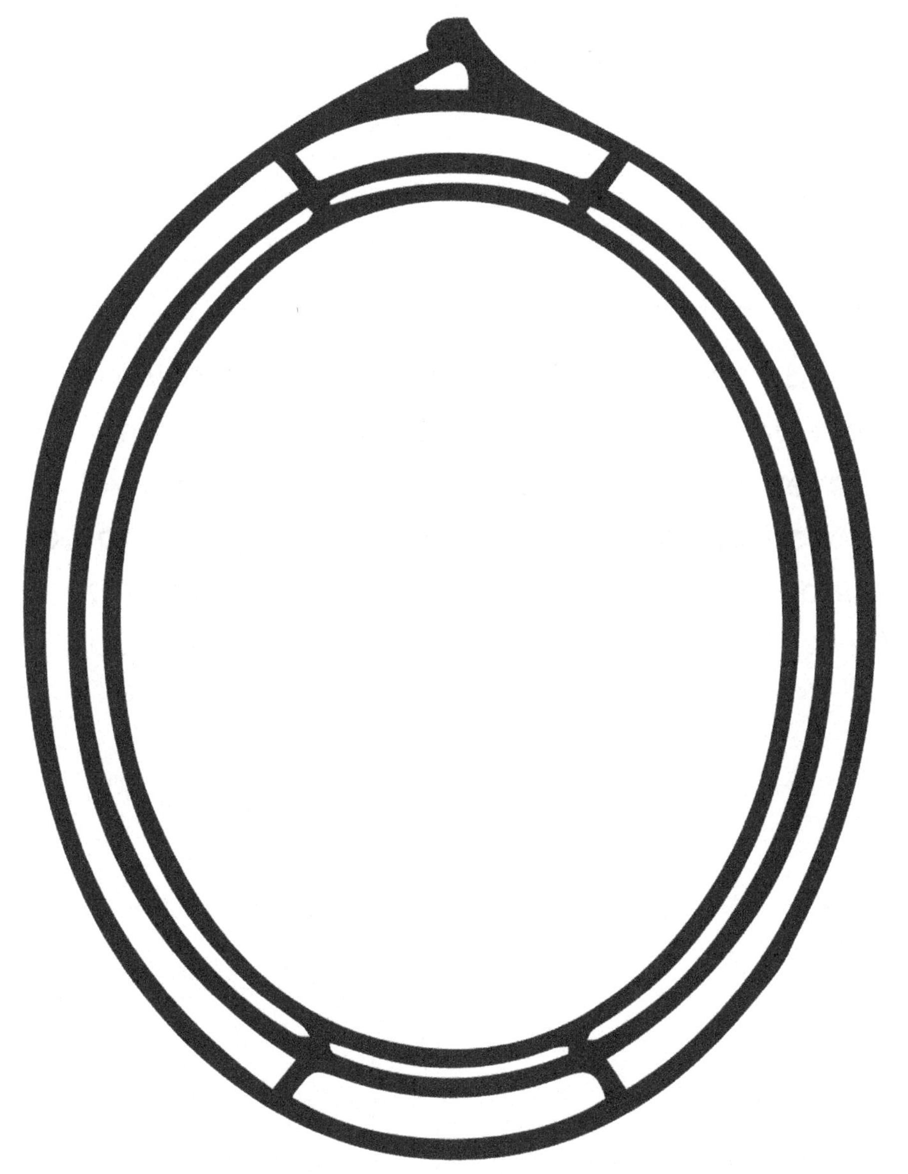

How do you think Fiona felt when she said, "One day, Melvin. One day we will be home forever with a real family, and every day will be wonderful." Is it possible for every day to be wonderful? What makes a wonderful day for Fiona? What makes a wonderful day for YOU?

Chapter 5
It's Been A Good Day
Still Late July

The car ride to get to the shore was long, but it was worth it. Fiona lived in Virginia her entire life but never saw the ocean. The instant she set foot on the sand, she knew she *loved* it. Fiona had seen pictures, and she saw movies and read stories about it, but none of that compared to seeing it with her very own eyes. The way the water blended into the sky and the clouds mixed with the waves was simply magical.

And the sand! Some of the sand was hot. Too hot to stand on for more than a second at a time. But some of the sand was cool and soft, and it squished through Fiona's bare toes and tickled with each step. Fiona love it. She loved everything about it.

She found a shady spot nearby, close enough for Lorraine and Pete to still see her but far enough away that Melvin could come out of the sand bucket and sit on Fiona's leg without being noticed. She spread her towel on the cool sand and gave Melvin the go-ahead to leave his hiding place.

"Isn't it great, Melvin? The ocean is so pretty, don't ya think?" Fiona asked. Poor Melvin covered his eyes with his tiny paws and hunkered down close to the sand. Turned out Melvin did not love the beach as much as Fiona did. She could tell he especially did not like the seagulls flying overhead, likely because of the way they kept staring at him like he was their next meal.

"Oh, Melv. Don't be afraid. I won't let anything bad happen to you. Just stay close to me. You'll be all right." Fiona promised.

One at a time, Melvin lifted his paws from his eyes. He stood tall on his back legs and sniffed the salty air, then fell flat on his back and rested in the sunshine. Fiona giggled. Just another thing she loved about her dearest friend. He always knew how to make her laugh.

Fiona and Melvin worked hard all day on a sandcastle they were building. Melvin was still quite nervous about the seagulls, but he did his best to help. He was good at smoothing the walls with his gentle, mole touch. It was hard work, though, and Fiona was getting frustrated.

"Ugh! Melvin, watch out!" Fiona scooped him up just as the castle's watchtower came crashing down. "I'm ready to quit this stupid thing. No matter what we do, it keeps falling down. It won't work! Why does everything have to be so hard?" she asked Melvin.

Fiona was mad. She threw down the shovel and stared at the water crashing against the shoreline, the white foamy stuff gathering and getting closer to her with each wave. *Maybe someday, if I ever get one, my real dad will build the biggest, bestest, most fanciest sand castle the world has ever seen,* Fiona thought.

"Hey, Fiona!" Pete hollered as he made his way over to her. He'd been watching from a distance and could see she was struggling. "Mind if I join you? I'd love to help." She wanted to accept his help, wanted to trust him and let him in, but she wasn't ready. Not yet, anyways. Besides, Melvin couldn't hide under a bucket too long in this heat. She couldn't risk Pete finding him.

"No, thank you. I'm okay." She could see that Pete was disappointed, and she honestly felt bad. But what choice did she have? She had to protect Melvin. She had to keep him a secret. There was no other way around it. Pete just waved and turned to go back in the direction he'd come from. Lorraine and Clyde were in the water, so Pete sat his chair—a little closer to Fiona than he was before. And there he stayed, reading his book the entire time she played in the sand, making silly faces at Fiona every time she glanced his way. When Pete stuck his tongue out at her, Fiona giggled. When he crossed his eyes and blew out his cheeks, she laughed. When he pretended to fall out of his chair in slow motion, acting afraid of the sand, she really, really laughed.

Fiona was sad when it was finally time to pack up and leave, but she was tired and she welcomed the coolness of the air conditioning in the car. It was a great day followed by a quiet ride home. Even the radio was quiet in the background. Fiona may have even drifted off to sleep a time or two. She closed her eyes and thought about their beach trip. Clyde and Lorraine hardly left the water except to eat lunch, Fiona and Melvin eventually finished their sandcastle, and Pete managed to finish his book even though he was being silly.

About halfway home, Pete flipped his turn signal, pulled off the road, and parked in front of a multi-colored ice cream shop. The red paint was peeling off of the gutters, and the tables looked sticky, but the line was still long, and the parking lot was full.

"I need a break." Pete handed Clyde a twenty-dollar bill and gestured toward Fiona. "You two can order. I'll have a strawberry shake."

"And I'll have the same!" Lorraine chimed in.

Clyde didn't hesitate to jump out of the car and get in line. Fiona followed.

"Get whatever you want, Fiona. Dad won't mind," Clyde said with a grin.

When the clerk came to the window, Fiona ordered the biggest Double Chocolate Chip ice cream cone they had, with rainbow sprinkles. She smiled at Clyde. *How exciting!*

"I'll take the same," Clyde told the girl at the window. He winked at Fiona.

What a weirdo. Fiona rolled her eyes and stuck her tongue out him. As they waited for their order, she looked down at her shoes and smiled to herself. It had been a good day.

Draw Fiona's sandcastle.

Pete noticed Fiona struggling to build her sand castle and offered to help her. Fiona declined his offer, even though, deep down, she wanted to accept. Other than to protect Melvin, why do you think Fiona turned Pete away?

Pete respected Fiona's request but continued to engage her with silliness from his seat. How do you think that made Fiona feel? How do you think Pete is feeling about Fiona now?

Chapter 6
Pushing the Limit
August

The pears on the tree in the Olivers' backyard were plump and ready to be picked. Every day, Fiona noticed more fruit on the grass below than what was there the day before. Somehow, summer faded into fall without warning. And everyone knew that the beginning of fall also meant the start of school.

Tomorrow, Fiona was starting third grade at Hoperidge Elementary School, which was not far from the Olivers' house. She was no stranger to new schools. Many kids in **foster care** change schools almost as often as they change underwear. Fiona was no exception. Starting a new school was something she had done many times.

How many times?

Five times.

Five new schools before the second grade.

Can you imagine?

"I wonder what school I'll go to after Hoperidge?" Fiona asked Melvin. He wiggled his nose, ran up Fiona's arm, and hopped into her pocket. Lorraine was already waiting for Fiona in the car, so they needed to hurry. They were going shopping today. Apparently, according to Lorraine, it was a required part of the process.

"You can't start a new school year without new school clothes." That's what Lorraine told Fiona last night, anyway.

Fiona really didn't think it was necessary to buy a new wardrobe just because of school. She would rather wear her overalls every day than spend even a minute in a dressing room. But Lorraine was so excited and insisted they go. Fiona reluctantly agreed. She could pick out an outfit or two to get Lorraine off her back. But she drew the line at new shoes.

Her red sneakers were the best. They slid right on her feet with ease, no tying or untying required. Mrs. Jones bought them for her brand new when Fiona was staying with Max and Joni. It took a while to break them in, but they are perfect now, and Fiona loved them. She spent a lot of time looking down at those sneakers, and she wouldn't be trading them in for another pair any time soon.

"Time to have some fun!" Lorraine exclaimed after their short drive to the mall. She opened Fiona's car door. *Fun?* Fiona wasn't so sure.

Once inside, they glided up a set of escalators, walked past the men's clothes, through the perfume section, and around the baby strollers on their way to the girls' clothing department. So far, Fiona wasn't having much fun at all. Melvin wasn't either.

"All right, Sweets. Let's do some shopping!" Lorraine said. Fiona wasn't sure how she felt about being called Sweets. "Pick out some things you like, and we can go try them on, okay?"

"Okay." Fiona half smiled on the outside but cringed on the inside. She grabbed the first few things she found on the rack and handed them to Lorraine. "But no shoes, right? Like you said?

"I don't know, Fiona. I guess I don't understand what the harm would be to have an extra pair to fall back on. Maybe something a little fancier for when you dress up? I think you should at least look, don't you?" Lorraine replied.

Fiona felt her face grow hot. Lorraine promised her she wouldn't push her to replace her sneakers.

She promised! She'd lied! "You said I wouldn't have to buy new shoes. You said you wouldn't make me. I don't care what you say about my sneakers. They're mine, and I won't get new ones!" Fiona yelled, hot tears running down her cheeks.

She'd never yelled at Lorraine before. She never really yelled at anyone. Especially not in the middle of a shopping mall. Fiona ran to a nearby bench. *If she wants me to have new clothes so badly, she can pick them out herself.* I'm done! she thought. Melvin stuck his tiny nose out of Fiona's pocket and peeked around. She knew he hated to see his friend so upset.

"Fiona, may I please sit down?" Lorraine pointed to the seat next to Fiona and sat down gently. "I owe you an apology. I promised you wouldn't have to buy new shoes, and then I pressured you anyway. I was wrong to do that to you. Do you think we can start over, Fiona?" Lorraine reached for Fiona's hand. "I'm having such a great day getting to know you, just us girls. I don't want it to end on a bad note. I promise not to pressure you to get new shoes again. Can you give me another chance?" Fiona wiped her tears away and took Lorraine's hand in hers. She wanted to leave. She was dead set on stomping back to the car with her arms crossed the whole way. But something about the way Lorraine looked her dead in the eye made Fiona believe she was actually sorry. Fiona couldn't remember a time when any of her **foster parents** apologized like Lorraine did. At least, she couldn't remember a time when she actually believed them.

Conversation during lunch was still limited, to say the least, and the rest of the day wasn't much better. This shopping trip proved to be a lot less fun than Lorraine had promised. Two hours and five stores later, their bags were overflowing. Fiona had everything she could possibly need to start the school year. Everything except a new pair of shoes. It wasn't Fiona's best day, ever. But it wasn't her worst, either.

That night, Fiona and Melvin curled up in their corner thinking about the first day of third grade and wondering what to expect. Tomorrow would be here soon, and Fiona would be the new girl in school. Again.

"I sure hope the third graders at this school are nicer than the second graders were last year. Don't you, Melvin?" She stroked his soft fur and scratched gently behind his right ear. If Melvin were a cat, he would have been purring.

Minutes later, Melvin was out like a light, but Fiona was still wide awake. She was physically exhausted but her imagination wasn't sleepy yet. With closed eyes, Fiona could see her future perfect family clear as day. Her imaginary new mom and dad sat on either side of her bed, her very own bed. Fiona snuggled in close between them. Her imaginary mom stroked her hair as her imaginary dad read her a bedtime story about fairies and goblins and magic spells that turned every person in the entire kingdom into circus clowns. Then they kissed her goodnight, wished her good luck for her first day of school, and left her room, closing the door behind them.

Like she did so often, Fiona fell asleep that night dreaming about her imaginary forever family, whoever they may be.

By second grade, Fiona has attended five different schools. How many schools have you attended? If you have had to switch schools, how did you feel on your first day as a new kid? Was there anything or anyone that made the transition easier for you? If you have not switched schools, how do you think it would feel to be a new kid? How have you tried to make a new kid feel welcome?

Lorraine made a big mistake. She broke a promise to Fiona, and Fiona did not take it well. Still, Fiona forgave Lorraine. What did Lorraine do to help mend the damage she caused? Why is Fiona surprised by this?

Chapter 7

Third Grade, Here I Come

Still August

Drip.

"Fiona!" Lorraine knocked on the door.

Drip. Drip.

"Wake up, Sleepyhead!"

Drip. Drip. Drip.

Raindrops tapping on the window made Fiona want to stay snuggled under her blanket. Today was the day. It was time for Fiona's first day at Hoperidge Elementary School. Fiona stretched her legs out straight and rubbed her tired eyes before she pulled herself up to look in the mirror above the dresser. *Yikes! Bedhead!*

Fiona reached for her brush and almost spilled the vase sitting next to it on her dresser. What is this? she thought. A single pink carnation stood upright in a thin crystal vase. Beside that lay one of Fiona's brand-new outfits folded nicely. A note on top read:

Dear Fiona,

Today is your day. Be brave and kind and happy today. You are so smart and so strong, Fiona. You can be whoever you want to be, and we will be proud of you no matter what. Have a great first day of third grade. We can't wait to hear all about it.

Love,

Pete and Lorraine.

Love?

Love.

Fiona smiled.

She folded the small piece of paper carefully and placed it in her sock drawer where it would be safe. She shut the dresser drawer and looked up at her crazy hair in the mirror once more.

"I can be anyone I want to be today, Melvin." Fiona liked the sound of that. "But not with this hair!"

Fiona brushed her hair and pulled it back with her red headband.

She brushed her teeth.

And got dressed.

With Melvin safe inside the front pocket, Fiona tossed her backpack over her shoulder and ran down the stairs for breakfast. Lorraine and Pete were waiting for her in the kitchen. Clyde was already gone—since he was in high school, he left earlier.

"Have some oatmeal, Sweets. Then Pete and I will walk you to school." Lorraine handed Fiona a bowl of oatmeal with a heaping scoop of brown sugar sprinkled on top and some raisins mixed in. Fiona ate the entire dish and then went to the door to put on her favorite sneakers. Pete and Lorraine followed. They didn't have far to go. Just up the main road a bit, one right turn and two lefts. Soon enough, they were standing in front of the school, umbrellas dripping.

Just a short way up the sidewalk, and Fiona would officially be the new girl in third grade. Her stomach was flip-flopping again. *I hate this*

part, she thought. Fiona reached over and grabbed Lorraine's hand. She squeezed it tightly, and took the first step. They walked together, slowly, never letting go of each other's hand. At the door, Lorraine knelt down to look Fiona in the eye.

"You got this, Fiona. Hold your head up high and be brave. Pete and I will be waiting right outside to walk you home when the day is over, we promise. Now go show this school how amazing you are." Lorraine gave Fiona a big hug.

And for the first time ever, Fiona didn't stiffen and pull away.

Draw **YOURSELF** on the first day of school.

In their note, Pete and Lorraine told Fiona she can be whomever she wants to be. Fiona liked the sound of that. What about you? Who do you want to be?

Lorraine hugged Fiona, and Fiona didn't pull away from her. What do you think that means? Do you think Fiona is becoming more comfortable with the Oliver's?

Chapter 8
The Stand Off
Late October

Each day was a bit easier than the last at Hoperidge. It wasn't long before Fiona stopped feeling like the new kid and began to feel more comfortable. She memorized the layout of the place pretty quickly. She knew where all the bathrooms were because she had to sneak into a stall as often as she could to check on Melvin. She knew where the nurse's office was because she fell at recess one day and skinned her right knee. And she knew where Tommy Taylor puked in the hallway that same day after lunch. She avoided that spot at all costs. All in all, it wasn't so bad.

It was usually too hot in her classroom.

The cafeteria food was mostly not horrible.

The kids were pretty cool.

And the teachers were nice, too.

With one exception.

Mrs. Jenkins, Fiona's homeroom teacher, was that exception. Fiona spent most of her school day in homeroom, sitting at her desk in the back row, studying Mrs. Jenkins from afar. The lady rarely laughed and never made a joke or teased. Hours could go by without so much as a smile. Mrs. Jenkins was the most serious, most uptight, most boring teacher. Ever.

Fiona tried to pay attention. Honest, she did. Still, the minutes grew longer, and Mrs. Jones's monotone voice grew more annoying. And Fiona's eyes grew heavier, and her yawns came quicker. Rather than fall asleep, Fiona doodled. She spent her time doodling little pictures of Melvin on the corners of all her papers. She was actually quite good at it. Until she got busted.

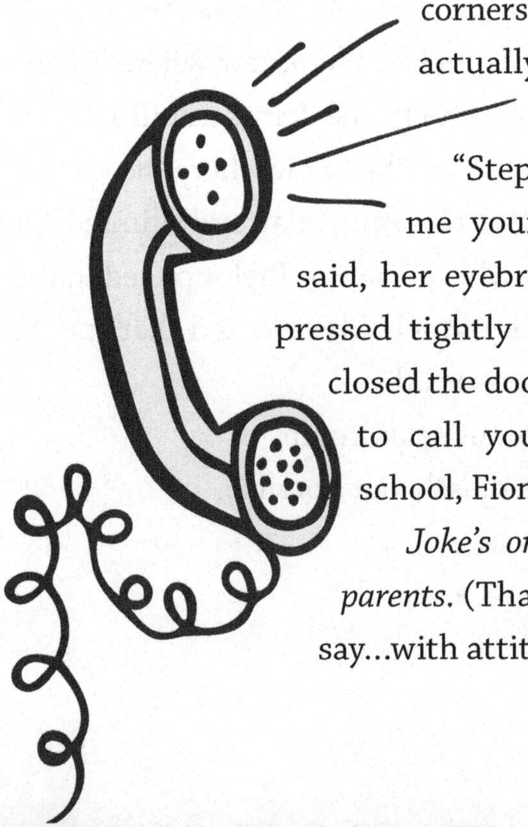

"Step out in the hallway with me young lady," Mrs. Jenkins said, her eyebrows raised and her lips pressed tightly together. Mrs. Jenkins closed the door behind them. "I intend to call your parents today after school, Fiona."

Joke's on you, lady. I don't have parents. (That's what Fiona wanted to say...with attitude.)

"Yes, ma'am." (That's what Fiona said...with no attitude.)

"You must take your school work more seriously, Fiona. It's almost November. You've been here long enough. Your adjustment period is over, young lady. I expect you to pay attention in my class, and you absolutely must finish your homework." Mrs. Jenkins continued. "You're a smart girl, Fiona. You must apply yourself if you want to succeed." Fiona traced the outline of her shoes with her gaze, keeping her toes centered on the brown floor tiles she was standing on, careful not to touch the grout.

"Go in and sit down. And try to pay attention." Mrs. Jones ordered.

When she opened the door, all the kids stared at Fiona with wide eyes. Whenever a teacher took a kid out to the hall, they were in trouble. To third graders, this was a big deal. Fiona sat down at her desk. She drew the cutest little top hat on her drawing of Melvin's head while Mrs. Jenkin's finished the math lesson.

That evening after dinner, Pete asked Fiona to sit back down in the chair next to his. She sat, shoulders slumped, arms crossed. *Here it comes. Time for the lecture.*

"You and I are going to go through your backpack tonight, and I will help you finish all the late homework assignments you have in there. Mrs. Jenkins is giving you an extra night to complete them, but you have to turn them in tomorrow morning. Please go get your backpack. Now."

Fiona stood still, staring hard into Pete's eyes. She wanted to challenge him, to dare him to make her. To prove to him he wasn't her boss. She wanted to go play with Melvin. She absolutely did not want to do a pile of homework; tonight, or any other night for that matter. The longer she stood there, the angrier she felt. Pete held her gaze. She could tell he wasn't going to give in.

Fiona ended their stare-off and stomped through the kitchen and up the stairs as hard as she could. She slammed the door with a loud thump and sat down on the edge of the bed, fuming. Her nostrils flared, and her breathing was heavy. Pete may win this battle, but she would make sure he knows just how unhappy she was about it. *The quicker I can make them kick me out, the quicker I'll find my forever family.* The family that won't ever give up on me, she thought. To Fiona, this seemed like the perfect opportunity to test Pete's patience. She grabbed her backpack and stomped all the way back to the table, each step louder than the last.

"Listen young lady. You can stomp and slam the door all you want. Yell, scream, pout...I don't care. I'll still be here waiting to help you, and we will most definitely sit at this table until the work is finished. Even if it takes all night." Pete was calm. He didn't get as angry as she expected. *Weird.*

Two hours passed, and they were just about finished. Fiona's mind drifted. She tried to think back to a time when any other adult in her life had helped her like Pete was doing. Miss Alice had always been kind to her, of course. But Fiona hadn't ever been this rude to Miss Alice. Fiona was trying her hardest to be a little snot, to make Pete angry enough to give up. Yet, here he sat, patient and understanding, working hard to help Fiona and getting nothing at all in return.

When the final page was complete, Pete stacked every sheet of paper into a neat pile and clipped them together. He reached across the table and gently held Fiona's hand.

"Look at me, Fiona." She looked up. "I am proud of you for working as hard as you did tonight. I knew you could do it. Thank you for letting me help you."

Pete walked into the kitchen and took out the carton of ice cream from the freezer. Fiona looked at the rooster clock on the wall hanging above the kitchen cupboards. It was past Fiona's bedtime, and she still needed to shower and feed Melvin. Pete slid an overflowing bowl of Double Chocolate Chip across the table and Fiona took a big bite. She snuck a chocolate chip into her overalls pocket for Melvin while Pete scooped a bowl for himself.

"What's another fifteen minutes, right?" he said.

Draw a portrait of Mrs. Jenkins.

It took a few months, but Fiona is beginning to feel comfortable enough to cause some friction in the Oliver home. Her "honeymoon" period is over, and it was time to show the Oliver's some real emotion. List some examples of how Pete responded to Fiona's tantrum correctly. Do you think Fiona really wanted to make him so angry he would make her leave? What do you think Fiona learned from this encounter?

Chapter 9
Horse, Meet Mole
Still November

The trees that were green and full just a few weeks ago were now left sad and bare. Piles of brown leaves littered the ground. A cool breeze hung in the air. Fiona pulled her sweatshirt closed and zipped it all the way up. Melvin climbed deeper into her pocket to hide from the wind. It was cold, but not too cold to be outside on their day off from school.

"What do you think we should do today, Melvin?" Fiona asked. Melvin looked at Fiona and then looked toward the basketball hoop at Clyde. He was dribbling his basketball back and forth in the driveway, looking just as bored as Fiona felt.

"We could go for another walk," Fiona suggested. Melvin stood on his hind legs and looked at Fiona. Then he looked at Clyde. Again.

"You're a silly mole, Melvin. Clyde won't want to play with me. He's probably waiting for Blake to come over." Fiona said, trying to convince herself it was stupid even to consider it. He wouldn't want to play basketball with a third grader.

Clyde was a nice enough kid, but he didn't bother with her too much. Like Fiona, he wasn't big on conversation. But Fiona had a feeling he was okay with her being there because he always made faces at her when Lorraine and Pete weren't looking. Like goofy, big brother faces. And he always winked after, as if to say he was just joking. *Hmmmm? Maybe Melvin's right. Maybe Clyde would let me play basketball with him.*

"Okay, since you insist. Wait for me in this flower pot, Melvin. I'll be right back to get you." Fiona put the pot in a sunny part of the porch where Melvin would be warm and safe, and then she walked over to Clyde. She fidgeted with her jacket the whole way, stopping short of the pavement and just standing there, her words stuck somewhere between her belly and her lips.

"Do you know how to play HORSE, Fiona?" Clyde asked.

"I don't think so," she answered.

"Come on. I'll show you." Clyde explained the rules of the game to her. "I'll take a shot at the hoop first, and if I make it, you have to take the same shot. You gotta stand in the exact same spot I was in and shoot it the exact same way I do. If I close my eyes, you have to close yours. If I shoot it backward over my head, you have the do the same thing, got it? If you try but miss, you get the letter H." Fiona nodded. She didn't really care what the rules were. She was just happy to be playing at all.

They played two rounds, and Fiona won both games. She was pretty sure he let her win, but she pretended not to know it. Someday she'd beat him for real, no doubt about that. Fiona loved the game, and she was glad Clyde taught her how to play. She secretly hoped that one day she would have her very own big brother that would show her cool stuff just like Clyde did.

"Can we play again?" Fiona asked Clyde.

"I think I heard Mom call for us. Dinner must be ready. Later?" He answered, and turned toward the house.

"Clyde, wait. I...um...I wanted to say I'm sorry. I didn't mean for your mom and dad to miss your basketball thing the other day. Sometimes, when I have to go to **court** for **foster care**, it takes a really long time." Fiona fidgeted with the zipper on her jacket.

"It's ok. Don't worry about that. You didn't do anything wrong." Clyde rustled Fiona's hair. "It'll be a different story if you make me stand out here until my dinner gets cold, though. I'm starving!" he rubbed his belly.

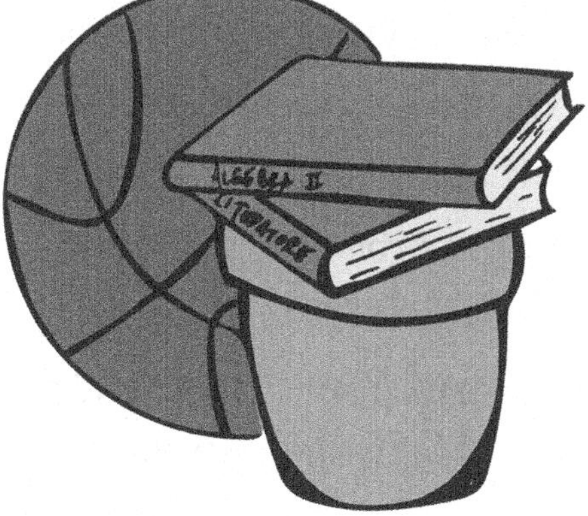

"Aren't you always!" Fiona teased and ran right past Clyde. She washed her hands and sat down at the table without a second thought.

Halfway through dinner, Fiona reached into her pocket to sneak her very best friend a piece of carrot and a small bite of chicken. The very best friend she forgot on the cold, dark porch! *Oh, no! Melvin!* Fiona panicked. She tried to think of something to say to get excused from the table. Fiona's mind went blank. *Just eat fast, Fiona.* Then go get him. She told herself. Fiona shoveled her food into her mouth as fast as her fork would allow. Her mouth was so full she could barely chew and when she took a drink of water to wash it down, some water dripped off her chin.

"Fiona, what are you doing? You're gonna choke." Pete warned.

"I mess I missed Billy Bugley," she mumbled, her words slurring together with all the food in her mouth. She swallowed it. "I guess I'm just really hungry." Fiona heard Clyde laugh under his breath, and then he caught her eye and nodded toward the door.

The flower pot.

Melvin's flower pot.

It was sitting on the floor of the entryway right beside Clyde's shoes with one of his giant textbooks carefully resting across the top like a lid. She looked at the pot and then at Clyde, her eyes as big as saucers, her heart beating out of her chest. Clyde winked and leaned over toward Fiona. "I saw you put him in there on the porch. Don't worry. Your little friend's just fine," he whispered. Clyde knew about Melvin? And he didn't rat her out? *Oh please, please, please don't tell.*

Fiona swallowed another giant mouthful of food without choking. She sneaked a few bites into her pocket and then kindly asked to be excused from the table. *Don't worry, Melvin. I'm right here.*

Draw Clyde playing basketball.

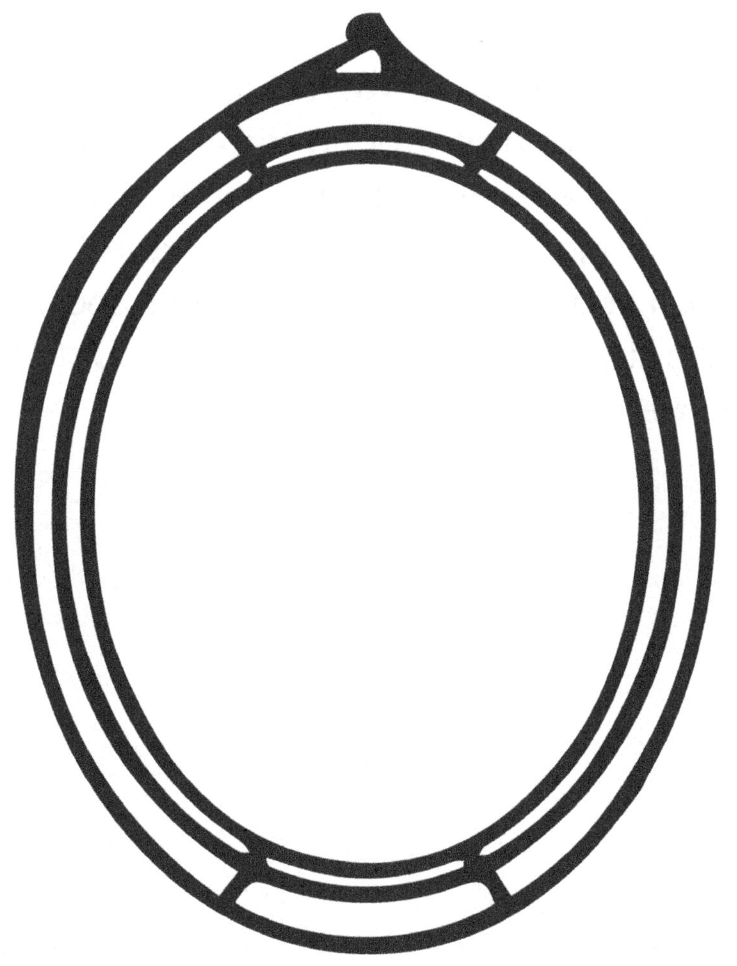

Let's talk about Clyde. We're finally getting a larger glimpse of a bond forming between Fiona and Clyde. How do you think Clyde felt about sharing his home with a child in foster care? Do you think he struggled with sharing his parents? How do you think you would feel if you were Clyde?

Chapter 10
Happy Birthday, Fiona!
December

Fiona turned nine on Thursday. You would think, like most kids turning nine, she would have woken up that third day of December bursting at the seams with excitement.

But you're wrong.

Fiona wasn't excited.

Birthday, shmirthday.

Just another day.

Fiona couldn't remember most of her birthdays. And the few she remembered, she'd rather forget. Her expectations for the day were low. Birthdays were for families and Fiona didn't have one.

Besides the casual Happy Birthday greetings from the Oliver's at the breakfast table before school, her day was like any other. There were no announcements made at school, no singing at lunch, no presents from friends. No one knew it was Fiona's birthday, and Fiona was okay with that. Being the center of attention made her belly ache anyway. She was happy that she made it through the day without a bellyache.

Or so she thought.

Outside, waiting for her when the dismissal bell rang, was Lorraine. With balloons. Nine balloons to be exact. Nine balloons, each a different color, floating high above Lorraine's head, waving in the wind for all the world to see.

"Oh geez. Look at those balloons, Melvin," she whispered. Fiona glanced around to see if her classmates were paying attention. She could feel her face getting red hot. She picked up her pace, silently praying that no one would notice.

"Happy birthday, Sweets! Hope you had a good day so far." Lorraine handed the bundle of string to a hesitant Fiona.

"Ummm...it was fine. Just like every other day." Fiona took the balloons and sunk down lower into her shirt.

"But it's not like any other day!" Lorraine exclaimed. "It's your special day!" She gave Fiona a squeeze. "Let's go celebrate!" Fiona forced a lopsided smile. She knew Lorraine meant well.

87

They started the evening at the local trampoline park, and everyone jumped until they could barely feel their legs. Melvin had to hang on for dear life inside the front pocket of Fiona's overalls. He almost flew out at least three times.

Lorraine started out jumping with the rest of the family but quickly tapped out. "I'm too old for this, guys. You three have fun. I'll take pictures from here."

"Mom pees her pants if she jumps too hard." Clyde whispered. Then he winked. Fiona giggled. And then they jumped as hard as they could for as long as they could.

"Our time's up in five minutes." Lorraine hollered from her seat. "Who wants pizza?"

They all got their shoes on and walked across the parking lot to Fachelli's Market.

"Anyone that knows anything about our little town knows about Fachelli's brick oven pizza. It's about time you see it for yourself, Fiona." Pete held the door open for her. "It's the best. Seriously. The best!"

Melvin would rather have had bacon, but Fiona *loved* pepperoni pizza and breadsticks more than anything. Fiona's eyes lit up when they entered the quaint pizzaria. Twinkle lights hung from the ceiling and a fancy-dressed man stood in the corner playing the violin. They sat in the corner booth near the rear of the restaurant, right beside the pizza oven. Mr. Fachelli gave Fiona her own little cup of dipping sauce for her breadsticks, and he let her watch him put the pizza into the brick oven. Fiona thought it was the best birthday dinner ever. She was so full by the time they left, she didn't know how she would be able to climb the steps to her room.

"Time for the cake!" Clyde messed up Fiona's hair, rubbing his knuckles over the top of her head as he barged past her into the house.

If I eat another bite tonight, I might pop! Oh, but it looks so good! She decided she would give it a shot. Lorraine lit ten candles on top of a gorgeous, double layer chocolate cake. One candle for each of Fiona's nine years and one extra candle to grow on. Pete, Lorraine, and Clyde sang the Happy Birthday song to Fiona, and she blew all the candles out with one breath.

She was raising her last bite of cake to her mouth when

Pete pushed her birthday present through the door. Into the kitchen rolled the shiniest, cleanest, brightest, most sparkly red bike Fiona had ever seen. A big blue bow was tied to the seat, and glittering streamers hung from each side. Pete rang the loud bell attached to the handlebars.

"Well, what do ya think?" Clyde asked.

Fiona's eyes widened, and her mouth fell open. She could hardly hold in her excitement. A big smile stretched wide across her cheeks, and her legs got wiggly.

"Happy Birthday! We hope you like it, Fiona." Pete smiled.

Like it? I love it! Fiona, speechless, looked up at Pete. Lorraine put her hand on Fiona's shoulder and gave a little squeeze.

"I can show you if you want me to. And we can take the training wheels off if you don't need them." Lorraine leaned down and hugged Fiona.

"I can ride it. I learned a long time ago." Fiona thought back to the day she found a rusty old bike piled deep under a bunch of junk in the garage. Her foster dad at the time, Ron, told her she could ride it in the back alley if she could dig it out herself. She did just that.

It took a few days and a few Band-Aids, but she eventually got the hang of it. Fiona taught herself how to ride, and she rode until the pedals finally fell right off that rickety old bike.

That was quite a long time ago, and Fiona had not been on a bicycle since. Nervous or not, she was ready to ride!

“Can we take it outside?” Fiona asked.

“Of course, silly. You can’t ride it in the kitchen.” Lorraine answered. “Zip your coat, though. It’s cold out there.”

Clyde carried her bike out the back door while Pete adjusted the straps on her shiny blue helmet.

“All set!” He slapped his hand on the top of her helmeted head. “You have the camera, Lorraine?”

Fiona ran outside as fast as her legs could carry her. Her bike was just beautiful! The way the red paint sparkled in the moonlight and the chrome wheels glistened—Fiona loved everything about it.

For the first time ever, Fiona had a birthday she would remember forever. She had a birthday she actually wanted to remember because everything about it was great.

Draw Fiona a birthday present from YOU.

The Oliver's showed Fiona she was worth celebrating. Why is this significant? What is your favorite birthday memory? If you don't have a favorite birthday memory, what would make your next birthday the absolute best?

Chapter 11
Accidents Happen
Still December

Fiona and Melvin had spent every spare second of the last four days riding her bike up and down the sidewalk, through the yard, and onto the driveway. Too bad she had to go to school. It was torture for her, seeing the sunshine outside her classroom, knowing her bike was waiting for her at home. She counted down the minutes while Mrs. Jenkins rattled on and when the dismissal bell rang, she high-tailed it back to the Olivers as quick as her nine-year-old legs could take her.

Fiona ran through the house, grabbed a snack and was back outside in record time, the screen door slamming loudly behind her. She caught sight of Lorraine in her garden patch pulling the dead plants, a large pile already sitting on the dirt beside her.

"Hey, Sweets! Slow down and tell me about your day. How was it?"

Fiona stopped running. "It was okay, I guess. Miss Jenkins gave us a pop quiz, and then Joni McGee lost a tooth. It was neat to look at even though it had some blood on it. She didn't even cry, and she cries over everything."

Lorraine cringed. "Sounds like you had an interesting day. Did you finish your homework?" Fiona nodded. *Crap. Homework. I'll do that later.*

"Pete took Clyde to basketball practice so we'll eat dinner a little late today. Stay close and listen for me to call you home, okay?" Lorraine said. Fiona nodded and shoved a few strawberries into her mouth and one into her pocket for Melvin.

Lorraine lifted her head, oversized hat and all, and waved at Fiona, just in time to see a big glob of strawberry juice drip from Fiona's mouth. They both laughed as Fiona wiped it with the back of her hand and ran to the garage to get her bicycle.

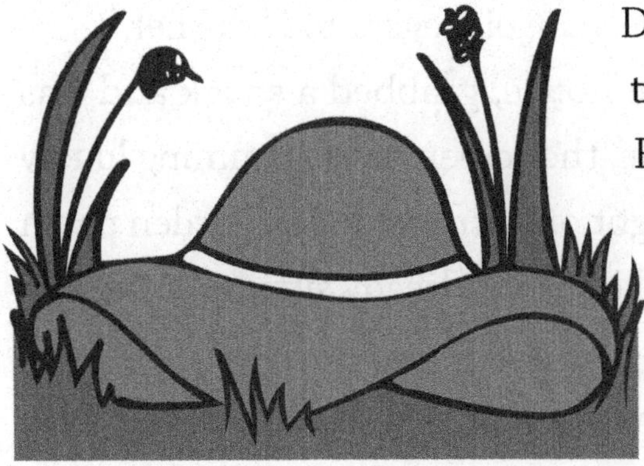

"I've been thinking, Melvin. I've been thinking that maybe our forever family will end up being a biker family. Don't ya just love to feel the wind on your face?" Fiona peddled faster. "Or maybe they'll have real-life motorcycles, and we'll ride down the highway going super-duper fast, letting the wind hit our faces so hard our cheeks jiggle."

Fiona closed her eyes and tried to imagine living with a bunch of bikers. With her eyes closed, she could see them clearly. Leather coats, black boots, and loud motorcycles. *Anything's possible*, she thought.

Fiona opened her eyes just a second too late. Her daydreaming had sent her pedaling right toward the neighbor's yard, smack dab into the fancy stone wall that lined their driveway. She

flipped over her handlebars and landed in a heap in the middle of Mr. Bugle's camellia garden. Melvin scurried out of her front pocket, unscathed, and hid behind a stone block. Fiona cried out. Her arm was hurting something fierce.

"Lorraine! Lorraine!" Fiona cried. She could see Lorraine running toward her through the grass. Her hat flew off her heard and landed on the ground nearby. Like a rocket, Lorraine was at Fiona's side.

"You'll be okay, Sweets. You're going to be okay. Let's get you to the hospital." Lorraine held Fiona's uninjured hand tightly and helped her up. Melvin made a mad dash up Fiona's leg and held on tightly while she walked to the car.

"Well, Miss Fiona, it appears as though your wrist is broken. Lucky for you, it's a clean break and we won't need to set it. What color would you like your cast to be?" the doctor said.

What color cast do I want? Is he serious right now? I don't care what color. I just want it to stop hurting. "Purple," Fiona answered.

"Good choice. Nurse Becky will be in soon. She'll have you fixed up in no time." He responded before leaving the room. *Nurse Becky? Why can't you just do it now?*

Fiona and Lorraine were still waiting an hour later. Apparently, Nurse Becky was taking her time.

"You girls in there?" A voice asked from behind the curtain. It was Pete.

Fiona was surprised to see them. "Is basketball practice over already?"

"It's almost over. We left when Mom called us and said you were hurt." Clyde answered. "Does it hurt real bad?"

"Not really. It hurt when I wrecked, but it's feeling better now." Fiona lied.

"Oh, honey. Can I give you a hug?" Pete sat on the edge of the bed and leaned over to hug her.

"You left practice for me?" Fiona looked at Clyde.

"Of course we did, silly. You're hurt." Pete stood up just as the curtain opened again.

"Hi, Fiona. Let's get this cast on you, alright?" *Nurse Becky, I presume? Nice of you to show up.*

The quiet nurse wrapped the wet plaster between Fiona's thumb and pointer finger and continued up her arm, stopping just before her elbow. Fiona thought it was neat the way it started out soggy and wet, molding perfectly to her broken wrist. After only a few minutes, it was hard as a rock.

"The pain will ease up when the swelling goes down. Until then, you must keep your hand up, like this." Nurse Becky held Fiona's arm straight up as if she was waving at everyone who passed by. "You're free to go home now but be careful with your wrist and be sure to keep the cast dry. And stay off the bicycle until the cast is off. You'll be as good as new in just six short weeks."

Hmmf. No big deal to you, maybe. Fiona didn't like Nurse Becky. Not one bit.

What a crappy day.

Draw Fiona on a motorcycle.

Fiona loves riding her bike. It's her favorite thing to do! Make a list of your five most favorite things to do for fun!

Chapter 12
Dear Lord, I Need Some Help
Late December

Sunday mornings at the Oliver house were for church. Fiona never went to church before in her life. She had a **CASA** volunteer a few years ago that told her about Jesus but she moved away before she could take her to a real church service. Fiona liked it. Especially since the Oliver's didn't dress up super fancy like she saw in the movies. Lorraine said it didn't matter what you wore, as long as you were clean, matching, and not wearing your jammies. Most

Sundays they just wore jeans. Sometimes Fiona would wear a dress. When she wore a dress, she always took a purse. For Melvin, of course.

Who cares that Clyde says Melvin can't come to church? The pastor himself said everyone's welcome. *Take that, Clyde!*

"Oliver Bus leaves in fifteen minutes!" Pete yelled up the stairs.

"Ugh! This will never work!" Fiona, frustrated, was unsuccessfully trying to button her dress. "Stupid cast!"

When Fiona broke her wrist last week, it was tough for her to accept Lorraine's help, especially for something as easy as getting dressed. Or brushing her hair. Fiona was used to doing things for herself. She hated asking for help. But she needed help. Again.

Reluctantly, Fiona called for Lorraine. Lorraine came, eager to help. "Do you think you could braid my hair again today, Lorraine? Can you maybe do two braids? One on each side?" Fiona asked shyly, while Lorraine buttoned the back of her dress.

"Pigtail braids! That's what my mom always called them. I'll give it a shot."

Although she'd never admit it, Fiona liked it when Lorraine brushed her hair. Lorraine never pulled too hard at the knots, she was gentle and it always looked pretty when she was done. Fiona really hoped her forever mom would brush her hair just like Lorraine did.

"Alright, Sweets. Is that what you wanted?" she handed Fiona the brush to put on the dresser by her mirror and left the room. Fiona looked at her reflection. She felt beautiful. She'd never felt this pretty before.

"Hey, Fiona!" Lorraine yelled from her room down the hall. "Come here for a quick minute and let me show you something."

Fiona put Melvin in her heart-shaped purse and swung it over her shoulder. Inside Lorraine's bedroom was a tall jewelry box with more jewelry than Fiona had ever seen. It sparkled like a pirate's treasure.

"I was thinking you might enjoy wearing a necklace today to go with your braids and your pretty dress. Wanna pick one?" Lorraine gestured for Fiona to choose a necklace. She lifted a shiny silver necklace with a little red heart charm out of the box. Red was her favorite color, and it would match her shoes. Lorraine helped her hook it in the back.

At church, during worship, when everyone sang together, Fiona slid the heart charm back and forth on its chain. While the pastor gave his message, she twisted it and untwisted it and then twisted it up again. And after church, when they were on their way to the grocery store, she traced the edges of the heart with her finger over and over again.

I wonder if my forever mom will share her jewelry with me, too?

Fiona does not like to ask for help. She likes to do things for herself. Have you ever been in a position to ask for help when you did not want to do so? Did someone help you? How did that make you feel? Why do you think it is so hard to ask someone else for help?

Chapter 13
Corrupted by a Cookie
January

Fiona knelt down in the hallway, just outside the double doors, as the stampede of students rushed by her on their way to lunch. Shielding her backpack with her body, she carefully unzipped the smallest front compartment. There, snuggled deep into the left corner, Melvin looked up at her with wide, beady eyes. He lifted his mousy paws towards her as if to say, *Let me out. I'm hungry.*

She reached her hand into her bag and felt him scurry up her sleeve to his favorite hiding spot. Fiona tried not to laugh. Now that her cast was off, Melvin's footsteps on her skin seemed to tickle even more than before.

Protected by her wild red curls, Melvin could sit on Fiona's shoulder and watch the kids without being seen. Not that anyone would notice, anyway. No one bothered with Fiona; not anymore. *Nice to meet you. My name is Fiona. Fiona the Invisible.*

Fiona didn't consider herself to be the new student anymore; too much time had passed for that. Still, she was alone. Being alone was safe. The fewer attachments she made, the less it would hurt when she moved away. It was better for everyone if she kept to herself. At least, that's what Fiona tried to tell herself. *Why bother making friends? I'll just have to leave them.* Melvin was enough.

"Aren't you, Melvin? You're the only friend I need." She whispered.

Fiona carried her lunch tray to her regular table in the very back of the cafeteria. She liked to sit at that table and look out the window at the parking lot. No one ever sat with her. *Just the way I like it.*

A couple of girls tried to sit with her at the beginning of the year.

"I like your glasses." One of them said.

"You're new, right? Where did you live before?" Asked the other.

Fiona didn't answer them. She just stared at her food, eating silently. They didn't come back to her table again. No one did. Until today.

"Hey. My name's Lou. What's yours?" Fiona never saw Lou

before, but she overheard Mrs. Jenkins talking about a new student this morning. *Lou must be the new student.*

"I'm Fiona." She answered and then took another bite of her buttered noodles. She adjusted her hair on her shoulder to be sure Lou would not see Melvin.

"I'm new here. Moved last week from Orlando. My dad got a new job, and even though my mom was super mad, he packed us all up and moved us up north. Even Teddy, our dog. Put him right on the back seat beside me. He puked three times in the car. It was the grossest thing ever! Thank goodness we had a lot of paper towels to....."

Fiona fake-smiled at Lou and looked back at her tray. *Share much?* She pretended to itch her neck and handed Melvin a pea.

"So, what do you do here for fun? Any parks? Amusement parks are my favorite, but swings and slides are fun, too. You go to the park, ever?" Lou asked.

"Um. Yes. I *have* been to a park before. There's one close to the school. I bet your dad will be able to find it." Fiona answered. *Does she seriously think I've never been to a park before? What's with this girl?*

"Well, maybe one day we can go play together. My mom said my only job today was to make one new friend. I think I pick you, Fiona."

"I'm not really much for making..." Fiona was about to say she wasn't much for making friends, but she got distracted by the tickle of tiny mole feet running down her back. *What in the world? Melvin?*

Melvin never ran off. He never showed himself. Ever. Yet, at this very moment, there he was making his way across the floor of the cafeteria. Fiona spotted him and did her best not to panic. *What are you doing you crazy mole?* That's when she saw the cookie. Fiona froze. She knew what her little friend was doing, and she had no idea what to do about it. She sat in her seat, eyes wide, heart pounding, and watched as Melvin took his first big bite.

"My dog, Teddy, is a tiny dog. He's a poodle. Do you have any pets?" Lou was still talking even though Fiona had barely said a word back. *Would you shut up already!* Fiona watched as Melvin took a second bite. She thought about getting up to go get him, but they weren't allowed to leave their seats until the bell rang to dump trays. *Just get back over here, Melvin!* He took a third bite. And a fourth. And then, just as he was lifting the last little piece of chocolate chip to his mouth, something terrible happened. Someone spotted Melvin.

Fiona watched in horror as her very best friend was covered by the looming shadow of James McBell, one of the loudest, most obnoxious kids in her class. She watched as James leaned over to get a closer look. Fiona held her breath when the boy reached his hand down to touch Melvin. And when Melvin looked up at James and squeaked, Fiona panicked.

“MOLE! “James screamed.

And Melvin ran.

Then Rosie screamed.

And Thomas Parks jumped onto the table.

The room erupted. (And Lou was still talking…)

Fiona watched as Melvin zigzagged through the cafeteria, between frantic feet, and under tables. *Where are you, now?* She couldn’t see him anywhere. Fiona got down on her hands and knees, desperately searching for her very best friend in the entire world.

“Melvin.” She whispered. “Melvin, where are you?” She was still crawling on the dirty cafeteria floor when Mr. Conrad’s whistle blew. All the kids sat down. The room went silent. No one moved an inch. No one except Fiona. She stood, slowly, and used her sleeve to wipe a hot tear from her cheek.

“Well, Miss Foster, it

seems you have some explaining to do. My office. NOW!" Mr. Conrad was not happy. Not happy at all. Fiona followed him toward the double doors, brokenhearted. She was worried about Melvin, worried she would never see him again. Until she spotted him, hidden against the door frame. *There you are! You little trouble maker.*

Fiona walked over to Melvin and knelt down in front of him. He jumped onto Fiona's hand and scurried to her shoulder as she continued through the doors. Mr. Conrad saw it. The entire cafeteria saw it. None of that mattered to Fiona as long as Melvin was safe.

Draw a portrait of Mr. Conrad.

Fiona referred to herself as "Fiona the Invisible." Have you ever felt invisible?

Fiona believes it's easier to push people away in the present in order to avoid losing them in the future. She would rather have no friends at all than risk the pain of losing them when she moves away. Can you think of anyone that you believe could benefit from having a friend? Can you list five ways to be a good friend to someone?

Chapter 14
Lost and Found
The Same Day in January

Fiona couldn't stop crying. She was so angry and so sad and really, really scared. After Mr. Conrad yelled at her for bringing a mole to school, he demanded she release poor Melvin outside in the grass along the edge of the weeds.

"Please, Mr. Conrad. I promise I won't let him out of my bag for the rest of the day. I promise I'll never bring him back to school ever again. He'll be so cold outside." She sobbed.

"Young lady, that dirty little thing has no business being anywhere but in the wild. January in Virginia is plenty warm for that rodent. It's a pest, not a pet. Now put it down and go inside to wash your hands. It's hard to say what kind of diseases that rat is carrying." The unreasonable man looked down at Fiona, his eyebrows pointed, his hands on his hip.

"Move it!" he barked.

Fiona knelt down along the weeds and whispered, "Melvin, I have to leave you here for now. But I'll be back. I promise I'll be back for you. Wait here, under this little log. I promise I'll be back as soon as I can." She brought Melvin up to her face. He squeaked a little squeak and rubbed the tip of his nose against the tip of Fiona's. Then he jumped down into the tall grass and hid under the log, just like Fiona had instructed. *Please, God, watch over Melvin while he waits for me.*

Fiona turned to face Mr. Conrad. She was mad. Livid, really. If she were a color, she would be the color of a hot poker, straight out of the fire, burning up. That's how mad she was. And she made sure Mr. Conrad knew it.

"I will never like you." Fiona's words spit out like sharp arrows. "I will never listen to you again. I hate you!" She tromped past the heartless man, slamming the door shut behind her, leaving him to open the door for himself.

"Don't you worry, young lady. You don't have to like me. Most of you kids don't. I'll still be calling your parents this afternoon. I'm going to tell them all about your little friend and the trouble you caused here today. I bet if they knew about that rodent they would have done the same as me. Just wait till you get home. You'll see!" Mr. Conrad yelled.

Too bad I don't have parents ya big jerk! Fiona thought to herself. *And too bad I won't be going home.* Leaving the Oliver's wasn't going to be easy. The thought of it made Fiona a bit sad. But she was there longer than she expected and it was time to move on.

Fiona spent the rest of the afternoon devising her plan. At the end of the day, Fiona would casually exit through the back door, the same door Mr. Conrad led her through with Melvin. Fiona would find Melvin and take him somewhere far away from Hoperidge Elementary School. Far away from mean old Mr. Conrad. Together, they would find a safe place where no one would ever take Melvin away from her again.

Fiona could barely stay in her seat while the school secretary read the afternoon announcements over the loudspeaker. When the dismissal bell rang, Fiona was out the door and at the tree line within seconds.

"Melvin?" She called out quietly. "Melvin, are you here?" Fiona was getting nervous.

What if he didn't wait for her? What if something hurt him? Or worse? "Melvin! Melvin! You come out here right this instant. Melvin!" She got down on her knees to get a better look, panicked.

That's when she spotted him. Melvin's poor little body was shivering wildly. Not from the cold, mice don't mind the cold. Melvin was terrified. He was curled up against the inside of the log, his tiny paws covering his ears and his eyes shut tight.

"Oh, Melvin. There you are. Don't be afraid. It's only me." Fiona picked him up gently and held him close to her. And then she ran. Fast. Fiona wanted to get as far away from Hoperidge as she could. All that mattered now was Melvin, no amount of guilt or fear would stand in the way of her protecting him. Even if that meant walking away from the Olivers and the first home she was starting to feel connected to.

Fiona and Melvin kept running. They ran through the schoolyard and down Main Street, past the post office and through the gazebo. They crossed the highway and ran behind the old tire factory and through the woods on the other side. They slowed down when they got to the Yellowbeck River and followed the walking trail, only stopping for a quick minute to rest. Melvin was quite comfortable hitching a ride in Fiona's pocket, but Fiona was almost out of gas. Still, she kept going.

"What are we going to have for dinner, Melv?" The sun was fading fast, and Fiona was starting to worry. They had left with no supplies, no food, no money. "We need to find somewhere to hide for the night. I don't want to walk in the dark." She was weary and cold. "That park! Over there!" she pointed. "We can hide in the climbing tubes. No one will find us there." Fiona pulled herself up into the highest tube and tightened her jacket around her as best as she could. Melvin nestled close on her shoulder and squeaked.

"I'm hungry, too, Melvin. We can find something to eat in the morning." Fiona closed her eyes. "Just try to get some sleep." She did her best to stay calm—to remain strong for Melvin. She didn't want him to know how afraid she really was. *Please, God, if you're there, watch over us. We just want to go home.*

Inside the blue plastic tube, Fiona twisted Lorraine's necklace between her fingers and rubbed her wrist. Her cast was off but, every once in a while, her bone still ached. Fiona's eyes grew heavy, and she drifted to sleep. But not for long.

"Melvin. Melvin, wake up. Did you hear that?" She whispered. She could see the faint glare from a flashlight dancing across the outside of the plastic tube. The steps were getting closer; the light was getting brighter. Fiona was never so scared in all of her life. She couldn't decide whether to make a run for it or keep praying. *God, please don't let it be a bad guy. Please make them go. Please don't let them find...*

"Fiona!" the light was blinding. "Fiona! Are you alright?"

"Pete?" Fiona cried out. Pete reached into the tube, and Fiona took his hand. He helped her down and hugged her harder than she had ever been hugged before.

"Honey, what are you doing out here? We've been worried sick." He asked.

"We didn't know what else to do. We kept going until we couldn't go anymore." She sobbed. "He said you wouldn't let me keep Melvin and I couldn't let anyone hurt him and then I was out here all alone and it's so cold and I'm so tired and so scared."

"We? Who else is here? Who's Melvin?" Pete shined his light toward the playground.

Fiona was too ashamed to look at Pete in the eyes. She lifted Melvin from her pocket. "This is Melvin. My very best friend in the whole entire world. Mr. Conrad made me set Melvin free. But I had to save him. I had to." She rested her head on Pete's shoulder as he carried her to the car, her teeth chattering from the cold.

Pete buckled Fiona's seat belt and turned the heat to full blast. "We've been looking for you everywhere, Fiona. Lorraine is frantic, and I'm exhausted. Mr. Conrad told us about what happened in the cafeteria today. We'll talk about your mole in the morning. Tonight, I'm just glad you're okay."

"I'm so sorry, Pete." Fiona wiped another tear from her face. Pete pulled out and turned the car toward home, but Fiona was asleep long before they got there, curled up into a tiny ball around Melvin in the back seat.

Draw Melvin.

After being forced to set Melvin free, Fiona decided she must run away from Hoperidge and her current home with the Oliver's. She made the decision quickly, to protect Melvin. Do you think she was upset about leaving the Oliver's? Why or why not? How do you think the Oliver's felt when Fiona ran away? Do you think Fiona regretted what she did afterward? When have you felt like running away?

Chapter 15

Will I Stay or Will I Go?

Late January

That evening after dinner, Fiona and Melvin sat on a blanket in their favorite corner. They didn't spend as much time there as they used to, but Fiona felt safe in her corner, and with everything going on these past few days, she needed to feel safe.

Melvin was crawling on Fiona's hands, weaving back and forth between her fingers and jumping from one hand to the other. She gave him a tiny piece of a green bean, and he nibbled it right up. Fiona loved to watch Melvin eat. His cute little front paws holding his small morsels up close to his mouth, tiny teeth taking little bites while his whiskers wiggled. She could watch him all day long. She was still feeding Melvin when she heard a light tap on her door. Melvin scurried underneath the blanket holding another bean.

"Fiona, can we come in? We'd like to talk to you about something very important," Pete asked.

"Yes, sir." Fiona was sure they were about to tell her it was time for her to go to a new family. She's been expecting this conversation all day. *Here it comes. I'm finally getting the boot.* Lorraine sat down beside Fiona on the floor. She took Fiona's hand in hers but said nothing.

"Do you remember the day you first came here?" Pete started. "Seven months ago, a shy, angry, hurting little girl walked through the door of our house. Fiona, that was the scariest day of my life. I was terrified that we would never get along and I was sure we wouldn't be a good enough family for you. I think I was wrong about that, but what do you think, Fiona? Do you think we're all getting along okay?" Fiona nodded. Pete was confusing her. *When's he going to tell me I'm leaving?* "The other day, when you didn't come home from school, was one of the scariest days of our lives. We thought we lost you. Picturing you out there all alone, cold and hungry; we were terrified. We never want you to run away like that again."

"Sweets," Lorraine brushed a strand of hair away from Fiona's eye, "what Pete is trying to say is that we love you, and we want to know how you would feel about staying here, with us, forever." Lorraine's eye filled with tears. "We want to **adopt** you, Fiona. Do you know what it means to be adopted?"

"It means I would always live here, with you," Fiona answered.

"Well, yes. It does mean that you would always live with us. But it means a lot more than that. When a child gets adopted, that child becomes a legal member of the family adopting them. The **adoptive parents** are then responsible for taking care of the child, physically and emotionally for the rest of their lives. They become connected as a family forever."

Like my forever family, Fiona thought.

"Pete and I have been praying for you for years. We've been praying that God would send us another child, the child He made special for us, and He sent us you. We've spoken with Mrs. Jones, and she's been helping us to complete our **home study**. There's just one last thing we need to do." Lorraine continued, "The last thing we need to do is to ask you, Fiona, what you want. We know that we want to be your forever family. We want that more than anything. But what do you want, Sweets? Would you like for us to be your family?"

My forever family? Fiona was in shock. "Does this mean you want to be my mom and my dad? Like for real?"

This time it was Pete's eyes that filled with tears. "Oh yes, Fiona! This means we want to be your mom and dad. For real. We want that very much."

"So you don't want me to leave? You're not mad about Melvin?" Fiona asked.

"We definitely don't want you to leave, Fiona. Not at all." Lorraine smiled. "As for Melvin, we're still discussing what to do about him. One thing we know for sure is that you absolutely can not take him to school again. Keep him out of trouble for now, and we'll let you know what we decide after Pete and I discuss it. He can stay for the time being. Deal?"

Fiona said nothing at first. She was too busy thinking. All this time, Fiona had been dreaming of her forever family, wondering when it would be time to leave the Oliver's so she could meet them. All this time she couldn't wait to meet her real, forever family. How could she not have seen it all along? A giant smile stretched wide across Fiona's cheeks. She'd already met them.

"Deal. For all of it!" Fiona agreed.

Draw Pete and Lorraine.

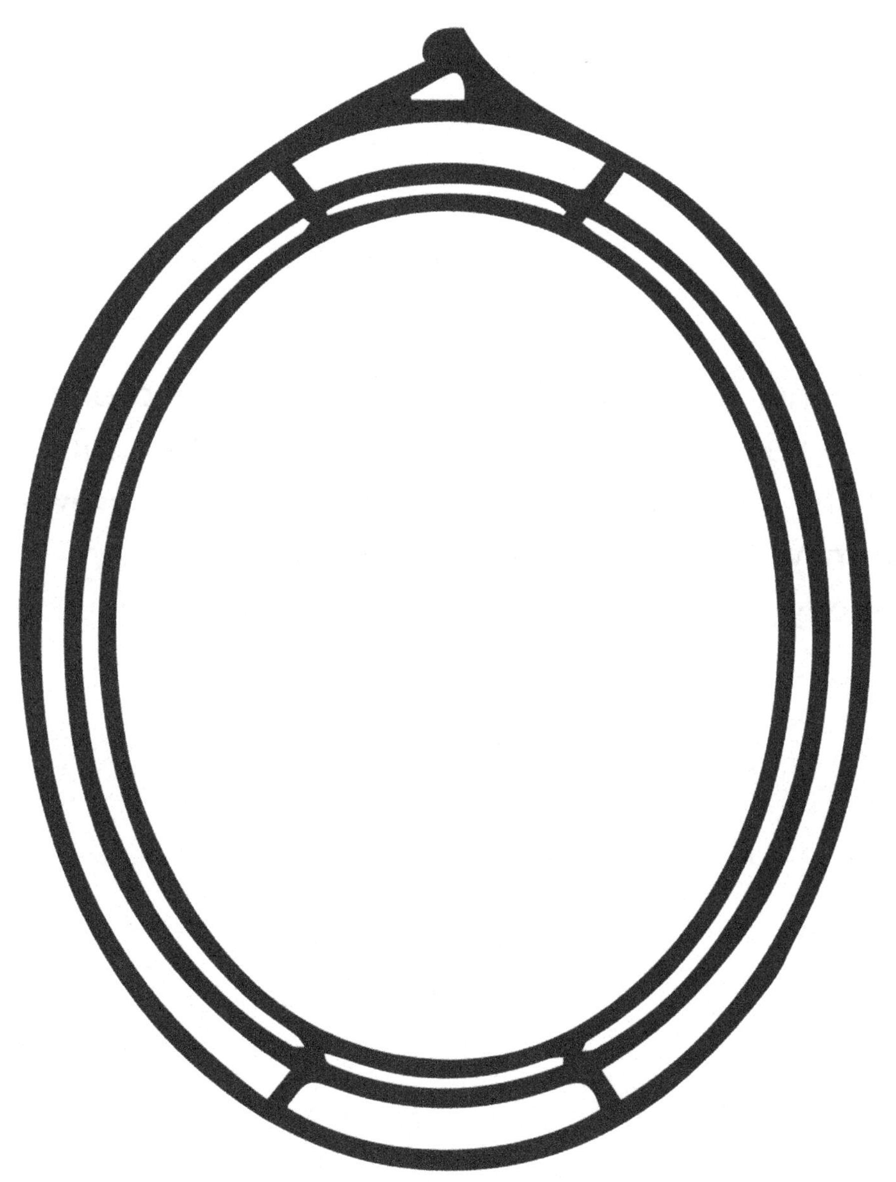

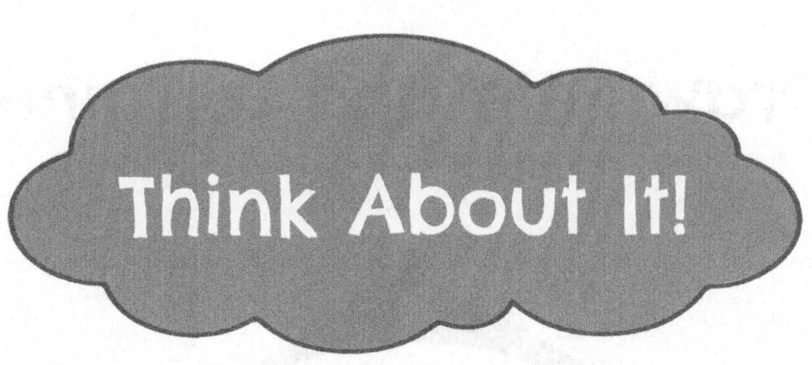

Up until this point, Fiona has continually dreamt of a new forever family. Why do you think she hasn't pictured the Oliver's as her future forever family? How do you think she felt when they finally asked her if they could adopt her?

Chapter 16

Forever, Finally

Early February

"Today's the day, Fiona! Our prayers have been answered." Mrs. Jones was at the courthouse when Fiona and the Oliver family arrived. She stood to greet them and gave Fiona a hug, then the double doors opened.

Fiona fidgeted with her purse. She was so nervous. This wasn't her first time in a courtroom. She had attended more **hearings** as a **foster child** than she could count. She was never nervous before, but this time was different. This was the very last time she would ever have to step foot through courthouse doors again. This was her **adoption** day.

Everyone that loved her was here with her,

even Melvin. He was inside her purse eating some dry cereal she had stashed in there this morning. They walked into the courtroom together. As usual, there were a handful of adults there, all dressed in professional clothes, whispering among themselves; yellow legal pads rested on the tables in front of them. Fiona's **guardian ad litem** smiled at her and the lady in front of the typewriter waved.

Fiona looked to the left. Someone in the back of the room caught her attention. "Miss Alice!" Fiona ran to the plump lady and hugged her tightly. "Miss Alice, you came!" She was thrilled to see her dear friend.

"Of course I'm here, girl. I been praying for this day since I first laid my eyes on those crazy red curls of yours." Miss Alice straightened Fiona's collar. "You best go sit with your family, now, girl. They's about to get started." Fiona hugged Miss Alice again and ran back to sit beside Clyde.

One man, the skinny older one with a gray comb-over introduced himself to Fiona and the Oliver family. "I'm Patrick Smithton, your **adoption attorney**. You must be Lorraine and Pete. It's nice to put faces to your names after so many phone calls." The grown-ups shook hands. Mr. Smithton turned to Fiona. "I'm assuming this pretty little lady is Fiona? How you doin', ma'am?" he ruffled her hair. Fiona smiled, but she was secretly annoyed that he touched her hair after she spent so much time brushing it that morning. "Time to get started." Mr. Smithton looked ahead.

"Please rise for the honorable Judge Lewis." The bailiff called the court to order. Judge Lewis sat up front, raised up high on his own miniature stage, his black gown hanging loosely over his body.

"Let me start by saying how refreshing it is to be here for such a happy occasion. Please don't be nervous. We are all here with the same goal." His eyes were smiling.

Lorraine was called to the stand first. She had to put her hand on the Bible and swear to tell the truth no matter what. She was so nervous that when she was told to raise her right hand and put her left hand on the Bible, she messed up and put her right hand on the Bible and lifted her left hand. She got flustered and everyone, even the **judge**, chuckled. Lorraine turned bright red.

"Relax, Mrs. Oliver. You're doing fine. Go ahead and have a seat right there." Mr. Smithton motioned her toward the witness box and began his questioning.

"Do you agree to take care of Fiona as you would a biological child? To provide all of her physical and emotional needs? To love her and be there for her no matter what?" Mr. Smithton asked.

"I do. In my heart, I am already Fiona's mother. I will love her, care for her, and provide for her like I do for Clyde. There is no difference in my eyes." Her voice cracked.

Next was Pete's turn. He figured out the hand on the Bible thing with no issues. Mr. Smithton asked Pete the same questions that he asked Lorraine. How old was he? What was his address? Where did he work? And so on.

"Do you agree to take care of Fiona as you would a biological child? To provide all of her physical and emotional needs? To love her and be there for her no matter what?"

Pete took a deep breath, "Sir, it is my honor and my privilege to be that little girl's daddy. Biological or not, she is mine, and I will do everything in my power to give her a healthy, happy, and safe life. I promise she will be well cared for and very much loved."

The judge thanked Pete for his cooperation and told him he could go sit with his family in the front pew. "And what do you think young man? Are you on board with all this?"

Clyde looked at Fiona and made an I'm-thinking-about-it-face. Then he smiled and winked at her. "Yes, sir. She's stuck with us now."

"And last but certainly not least, what about you, Fiona? How do you feel about the Olivers adopting you?" Judge Lewis asked.

When she tried to speak, she couldn't make any sound come out. Her emotions were stuck where her voice was supposed to be. Lodged in her throat was an invisible lump made of happiness and fear mixed with the pain of her past and the excitement of her future. So many feelings for one girl to handle, yet, Fiona handled it with grace. She cleared her throat and tried again.

"I haven't had a real family since I was a baby. I don't remember anything about them. I only know what I've been told. I have lived with eight different families in eight different houses, some of them I don't even remember. Some have been really nice. Some of them were mean. None of them ever felt like home. Until I met Pete, Lorraine, and Clyde. I love them, and I know they love me. Pete helps me with my homework and won't let me give up. Lorraine brushes my hair and lets me help her make dinner. Clyde is weird, but I think all big brothers are weird, right?" Judge Lewis laughed and Fiona continued. "For all my life I have never felt like I truly belong anywhere, until now. This is my family. Their home is my home. I finally found where I belong."

His Honor was smiling. "Well, that's good enough for me! Congratulations young lady. As of today, you are officially Fiona Lynn Oliver." He smacked his wooden gavel against the desk in front of him, and Pete and Lorraine hugged Fiona tight. And Fiona hugged them back even tighter.

When Fiona spoke in the courtroom, the emotions she felt got "lodged like a lump" in her throat, causing her words to get stuck for a moment. Fiona felt happiness and fear, mixed with pain and excitement. She was happy to be gaining a new family, perhaps a little fearful of the changes occurring, pained by the sadness of her past hurts, and excited to finally move on from that. Use this page to describe how this emotional chapter made YOU feel.

Chapter 17
Fiona's Room
Early February

After such a long and exciting day, Fiona's eyes were heavy. She was laying in her bed. *My bed. My very own bed. Not a borrowed bed. Finally.* She was petting Melvin between his tiny brown ears—he always loved that.

"Can you believe it, Melvin. We finally have a real family. I still can't believe it." Melvin wiggled his little nose, and his whiskers followed. Fiona was petting his plump, soft belly when the door cracked open.

"Fiona?" It was Lorraine and Pete standing in her doorway. They were carrying a long, narrow cardboard box.

"We have something for you, Fiona." Pete took a wooden sign out of the box. He also took out a hammer and a nail. Pete hung the sign on Fiona's door and then opened it wide so Fiona could see what it said. In bright red capital letters, the sign read FIONA'S ROOM.

"This is your room, Sweets. Our home is your home, and that will never change. It's just a simple little sign, but we wanted you to be reminded every day that you belong here." Lorraine continued, "And one more thing," she bent down and took something else from the box. "This is for your little friend. It's about time he's treated as part of the family, too." Lorraine handed Fiona a wire cage, complete with a water dispenser and an exercise wheel. "Throw out that stinky shoebox you have hidden under your bed and sit that cage right there on your nightstand. There's bedding and food here, too. You can set him up real nice."

"You mean I can keep him?" Fiona's mouth dropped open. "I'm really sorry for sneaking him in the house, but Melvin's my best friend. He's my family."

"Well, now we're all family. Including Melvin." Pete pulled the corner of the blanket up off the bed where Melvin was hiding. Melvin climbed onto Pete's palm for a quick second and then ran to hide behind Fiona. Pete and Lorraine giggled and stood to leave the room.

"Lorraine, wait!" Fiona said. "Do you think we can go to the mall tomorrow? I think I need some new shoes."

"Sweets, I'll buy you the entire shoe store if that will get you out of those red sneakers." They all laughed.

"Maybe I'll ask Lou to come along. She's new at school. Would that be okay?"

“I think that’s a great idea.” Lorraine said as she kissed the top of Fiona’s head.

“Goodnight, Fiona. We love you.” Pete gave Fiona a hug and a kiss next.

“I love you guys, too,” she responded.

And she meant it.

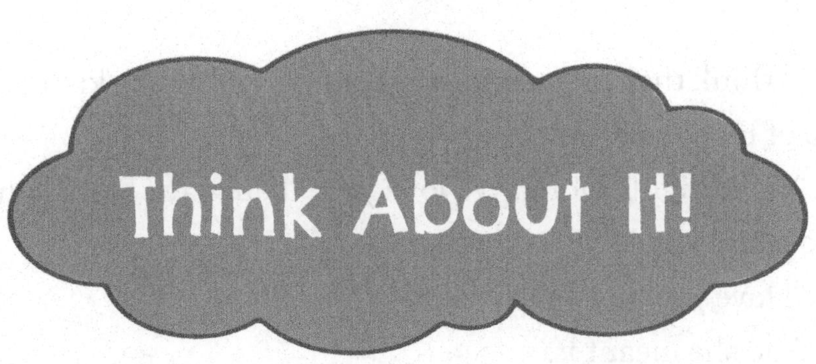

After months of sleeping in the corner of her room, curled up on the floor with Melvin, Fiona finally chose to sleep in the bed. Why is this important?

What Happens Next?

If you could write one more chapter after the ending, what would you write?

Glossary

adoption

The social, emotional, and legal process through which children who will not be raised by their birth parents become full and permanent legal members of another family.*'

adoption attorney

A lawyer who practices in the field of adoption law, and who has proficiency in filing, processing, and the finalization of adoption matters in courts having appropriate jurisdiction.*

adoptive parents/family

Persons who did not give birth to a child, but selected that child to be a member of their family. After a legal adoption, adoptive parents have all of the legal rights of natural parents.+

best interests of the child

The deliberation that courts undertake when deciding what type of services, actions, and orders will best serve a child as well as who is best suited to take care of a child. "Best interests" determinations are generally made by considering a number of factors related to the circumstances of the child and the circumstances and capacity of the child's potential caregiver(s), with the child's ultimate safety and well-being as the paramount concern.*

biological parents

Also referred to as the birth parents, they are the two people who [created] a child.+

bonding

The process of forming an emotional attachment. It involves a set of behaviors that will help lead to a close personal bond between the parent/caregiver and their child. It is seen as the first and primary developmental achievement of a human being and central to a person's ability to relate to others throughout life.*

caseworker

A person who works closely with youth and their families to provide services and support, with the goal of permanent placement for the youth.^

child protective services (CPS)

The social services agency designated (in most States) to receive reports, conduct investigations and assessments, and provide intervention and treatment services to children and families in which child maltreatment has occurred.*

CASA (court-appointed special advocate)

A person, usually a volunteer appointed by the court, who serves to ensure that the needs and interests of a child in child protection judicial proceedings are fully protected.*

family reunification

Refers to the process of returning children in temporary out-of-home care to their families of origin. Reunification is both the primary goal for children in out-of-home care as well as the most common outcome.*

foster care

A 24-hour substitute care for children placed away from their parents or guardians, and for whom the State agency has placement and care responsibility. This includes, but is not limited to, placements in foster family homes, foster homes of relatives, group homes, emergency shelters, residential facilities, child care institutions, and pre-adoptive homes.*

foster child

A child who has been placed in the State or county's legal custody because the child's custodial parents/guardians are unable to provide a safe family home due to abuse, neglect, or an inability to care for the child.*

foster parent

Adults who provide a temporary home and everyday nurturing and support for children who have been removed from their homes. The individual(s) may be relatives or nonrelatives and are required to be licensed in order to provide care for foster children.*

guardian ad litem (GAL)

A lawyer or layperson who represents a child in juvenile or family court. Usually this person considers the best interests of the child and may perform a variety of roles, including those of independent investigator, advocate, advisor, and guardian for the child. A layperson who serves in this role is sometimes known as a court-appointed special advocate (CASA).*

home study

The process of gathering information, preparing, and evaluating the fitness of prospective foster, kinship, and adoptive parents. The primary purpose of a home study is to ensure that each child is placed with a family that can best meet his/her needs. Home study requirements vary greatly from agency to agency, State to State, and (in the case of inter-country adoption) by the child's country of origin.*

judge

The head of the court who is responsible for listening to a child and others involved in his/her life. The judge makes decisions about what will happen to the child.[+]

kinship care

Placement of a foster child in the home of someone who is related to the child by family ties or by a significant prior relationship connection.[^]

hearing (permanency plan hearing)

A court hearing for all children in foster care that must occur shortly after coming into foster care and every 6 months after that until a child leaves foster care.[+]

TPR (termination of parental rights)

When a judge signs an order that permanently ends the ties between a child and his/her parents.[+]

[*] www.childwelfare.gov/glossary

[+] www.winfamilyservices.org/terms-and-fostercare

The definition of "biological parents" has been altered slightly for clarification purposes.

[^] https://www.fosterclub.com/glossary

Made in the
USA
Monee, IL

15760359R00095